Who's Afraid of Red

A Story Cycle in Three Parts

Alessandra Gelmi

PublishAmerica
Baltimore

© 2007 by Alessandra Gelmi.
All rights reserved. No part of this book may be reproduced, stored in a retrieval system or transmitted in any form or by any means without the prior written permission of the publishers, except by a reviewer who may quote brief passages in a review to be printed in a newspaper, magazine or journal.

First printing

All characters appearing in this work are fictitious. Any resemblance to real persons, living or dead, is purely coincidental.

ISBN: 1-4241-4866-9
PUBLISHED BY PUBLISHAMERICA, LLLP
www.publishamerica.com
Baltimore

Printed in the United States of America

Who's Afraid of Red is fiction inspired by true events. The Rwandan massacre was real. May the souls of the faithful departed, through the mercy of God, rest in peace. Amen.

# PART ONE
IN BED WITH THE TRUTH

January 1997
Sylvia and Leon
Washington, D.C.

"How can our two-milliwatt brains comprehend the universe?" she asked him. Nude, facing him in her bed, Sylvia added, "We exist only as adjectives for God."

She used the word *God* and not *higher power*—the latter being his preference, the latter ratifying his own manly potential.

He leaned over and kissed her. She kissed him back harder.

"I adore you," he said.

"You're too vain for that."

"For what?"

"For giving it up like that. For me, God, or anyone."

She pulled the bed sheet to her chin. Outside, ospreys cawed. The sun in the sky was a rag on fire.

He said, "I miss God."

She stood up, slipped on the silk chemise draped over a nearby chair, and walked toward a window. The morning light was thick, almost viscous.

"Ospreys are the bikers of the bird world," she replied staring out. "Blue-collar outlaws with attitude."

"I miss the times I was weak, but my faith was strong," he said.

She turned around and looked at him. "*Faith is a level of knowing,*" she said.

"Good old St. Augustine," he said, "never missed a party or a chance to get laid. Tempted by the flesh. 'O Lord give me continence and chastity but not just yet.'"

Sylvia grinned. "Seriously, Leon, you'd think if God knew you were going to abandon your faith, he would have made you another species, a bird perhaps. Birds are not interested in knowing. Not the way men and women are." She moved closer to him.

"I miss the passion," he said. "I miss my passion for God." He reached out from the bed, grabbed her knee, and bit it playfully.

"Bald eagles, on the other hand, are the lawyers of the bird world. They dress in power suits and build ostentatious nests," she said, clearly enjoying the attention. She climbed back into bed and rolled toward him. They made love again. Afterwards, he took her hands and pressed them to his lips.

"What are you thinking about?" she asked.

"Love," he answered, "what it feels like."

She brushed his lips with hers. "Does it feel real or imagined?" she asked.

"Things that feel too good to be true generally are," he replied. "Did you ever read Rudolph Otto's *Idea Of the Holy*?" he asked. "Required reading in a basic theology course. He was this German theosopher who—well the premise of the book was the idea of the *numinous*, what he called the *numinous*. *Numins*, the etymology's Latin, are spirits. Anyway, I remember being in the first pew of the cathedral in Padua, Italy. I was in my twenties. So fresh. And I remember hearing this reed-like soprano singing Mozart's *Requiem*. Nothing human had ever sounded so pure to me. I remember staring at these huge frescos; the starkness and majesty of the physical forms exploding from the canvas. And I remember losing it, probably because I was falling in love. I was so raw to something so inspired! For those few moments, the divine was mine. I fucking ached with love. Do I know what love feels like? Don't tell me I can't be seduced by mystery, that I'm too vain to adore another. I've been there."

Sylvia studied his hawk-like cheekbones, the Faustian fury in his eyes.

"Soaking up this love," he continued, "My loins were on fire. My mind was a white-blaze. This was it! Such a high!" He took a breath and exhaled slowly. "I was such a twit then! I would feel love everywhere. In trees, in envelopes, in a *Gauloise* cigarette and cup of good coffee! Everything was a blessing. Insults and transgressions too!"

She fixed on him now. Her intensity bordered on intrusion.

"Then I got smart," he continued, "once I realized God was a loan shark, that this faith, this love, this idea of the holy, wasn't a freebie but came with a price."

"What price?" Sylvia asked.

"You tell me." He broke his gaze. "Look, Sylvia, I'm supposed to leave for Rwanda. Follow-up coverage on the genocide I reported three years ago."

"You're leaving?"

"I can't believe I was actually *there*, in *Rwanda*. Before that, *Liberia*, reporting." The light in her eyes dimmed. He pressed his forehead to hers. He resurrected a memory.

"Liberia. Back and forth in the early 90s. Back and forth. What a stinking nightmare. I remember seeing guys in wedding gowns and blond wigs. Mickey Mouse and Donald Duck masks. Doing body art on each other, stoned on hallucinogens, painting their bodies not with ordinary paint, *but with the blood of Monrovian nuns*."

He reached over to the night stand for a tumbler of water and took a gulp, offering her the glass. She shook her head.

"Commandos with names like *Pepper* and *Salt*," he continued, "in dread locks and Nike Air-Pumps. And do you know what they were doing? Do you have any idea?" A look of disgust came over his face. He said, "They were playing ping-pong with a baby's heart."

"Leon, you sound so stoic! What's up with that?"

"'We want peace. We are not interested in killing innocents.' Lip service out of their goon-mouths."

"Why do you sound so impervious to this horrible stuff? You saw this?"

"What are you talking about?" Leon asked.

"You just sound so disconnected—as if you've pushed past events, people, even God away."

"Is that what you're doing to me right now?" Leon asked.

"What?"

"Pushing me away?"

"Why would you say that?" she asked.

He seemed to lose the thread of conversation and slowly began mouthing the lines of a Hart Crane poem he'd memorized as a boy: "…the red animal—war—the blood swollen god…"

"God didn't push you away from Him; you left," she said. She pulled the sheet down, exposing her nude body and turned toward him. He did not look at her. Finally she asked, "What do you hear?"

He turned to face her. "The wind?" he answered.

But there was no wind, only the frequencies of their thoughts. What it was he thought he heard, what she heard, what it was between a man and a woman, vibrations that disturbed the order of the day.

December 1996
Sylvia and Leon
Washington, D.C.

All the men at the party in Potomac, a wealthy D.C. suburb, had worn suits. He'd dressed in jeans and boots. *A plus,* Sylvia thought, *in contrast to the dull Washington norm.* She figured him to be around her age, mid to late thirties. His hair was black, thick, and long. He had inscrutable eyes and a square jaw.

"You must be a grinder," she said to him.

"Are you asking me to dance?"

"Your jaw is three times larger than normal for a man."

"Thank you; I'm built to please. What are you, a size six? Waist-to-hip ratio .70?"

"I said your jaw. It's not a compliment, just an observation."

"What do you do?"

"About what?"

"I thought you might be a dentist or a plastic surgeon."

"I'm a painter," she said, "though I stopped painting a couple of years ago."

"Why?" he asked.

"I just stopped producing work that communicated my trademark urgency."

He studied her and said nothing.

"*Sic transit gloria mundi,*" she said with a manufactured ennui she detested immediately.

She liked Leon. Something weather-beaten about his face gave him a mature edge, unlike the last guy she'd dated, who looked like a Naval Academy plebe.

"So how do you know Aldo?" she asked.

"We used to be neighbors when he was single and living in Bethesda. You?"

"Aldo negotiated a show for me in the lobby of the World Bank. He's a VP in charge of something there that has nothing to do with art. If you want the real skinny, it was a freak-show."

"Why?" Leon asked.

"The work was multimedia," Sylvia began. "I'd incorporated steel projectiles into some pieces. Apparently during the installation, an Afghani sitting in the lobby of the building was gouged by one of the projectiles. Poor guy was here on a peace mission. Ended up in traction."

"And you're groaning that people aren't moved by your work?"

His next question startled her, not because it challenged her own set of assumptions, but because it arrived so abruptly on the heels of a joke. "Do you think you had what it takes in the talent department, then lost it?"

"People don't lose their talent. They lose their inspiration. Leon…you said your name was Leon…"

He nodded.

"Do you mind if I call you *Jaws*?"

"Go ahead," he said.

"What else of yours is party size?"

Mocking herself for being ridiculously predatory she laughed at her own expense, then winked at him. He appreciated the fact she felt so comfortable with him. It was, he imagined, a subtle form of flattery.

By age thirty, Sylvia had won the attention of several distinguished curators in Manhattan. She'd received national awards and been profiled in art journals of note. She had been invited to teach at Yale in Art and Architecture.

Shortly after, she had lost interest in the trajectory of her career. Now at thirty-five, she found herself teaching studio art to manicured coeds at a pricey college perched on the District line.

If her life seemed small, she didn't know if she lived it this way because she liked the simplicity or because she wasn't brave enough to have gone for the brass ring. That ring dangled in front of her, and she hadn't grabbed it. Why? She wasn't sure a circus life—one high-wire act after another, a public persona she would have to parade, private time she would have to sacrifice, the fickleness of the downtown art scene, (one minute you were up, the next minute you hit the net)—was what she wanted. That life didn't seem rich. That life seemed rash.

The night she met Leon he informed her he'd covered the 1994 ethnic war in Rwanda, a war, he said, that "left more than half a million dead." He said he'd covered the Liberian conflict begun Christmas Eve in 1989 when "a monster named Taylor invaded from the Ivory Coast and killed 750,000 people in the next six and a half fucked-up years." He told her he had had it with war. That if faith was a level of knowing, war had dunced him. He needed a pointed hat and a chair in the corner for having been one of the faithful.

He told her after all these years he was ripe to the notion there was never a good war or a bad peace, that he had begun his career in the Peace Corps after attending divinity school and had begun writing monographs in Africa. Monographs eventually picked up by *The Washington Post,* leading to full-time work. That after two years, an editor from the foreign service desk had submitted his pieces to the Pulitzer jury, working foreign press members, who, eager for new blood in the ranks, chose him over a two-time-award-winning *New York Times* reporter.

Sylvia initially had eyed Leon talking to a slat-thin woman scooping *fois gras* onto a *Ginori* plate.

"Midnight Mass." Approaching them, she caught the last part of a sentence he spoke to a woman dressed in a dusk suit.

"Are you going?" Sylvia interrupted.

"I hate the Catholic Church," he said.

The ghost of a scowl crossed Sylvia's face. "What a novel attitude!" she said. Her eyes shone with impish verve. "Let's just say I respect the imagination of the doctrine," she said. "*The Virgin Birth, The Resurrection, The Ascension*! Who can imagine events like that? What's more, imagine them as true? I applaud such leaps of faith!"

"So you believe in Satan?" Leon asked.

"Didn't Baudelaire say the devil's greatest wile is convincing us he doesn't exist?" she answered.

"Excuse me," said the woman in the dusk suit, exiting.

"Heard he's flogged cupcakes lately," Leon said.

"Excuse me?" Sylvia said.

"*Devil Dogs*! In between junkets to Serbian death camps," Leon said glibly.

"Did you say flogged? What the hell are you talking about?"

"Were you?"

"Flogged? I was disciplined!" She tossed a lock of hair back with her hand, one flick. "You know, I absolutely love the Catholic Church, the archness, the rules. I wish I didn't love it as much as I do. Because, as John Simon once observed, when you love something you become more severe. Stupid people, when they love something, become indulgent and blind. But the thoughtful and discriminating become more demanding."

"Someone took a leather strap to you."

"It was Italian leather, soft as…"

"That's abuse; don't poeticize it," he said.

She looked at his rock-glass filled with half an inch of what looked like Scotch. "Do you poeticize your drinking?" she asked.

He ignored her question, took a sip from his glass, then laid it down. He buried his thumbs inside his front jean pockets, fingers framing his groin.

Very near them a matron in an Oleg Cassini print explained to her friend, "With a buffet you can mix politicians, artists, lobbyists, musicians; but with a seated dinner, I've discovered that the guests all have to be from the same milieu, so they know each other a bit. Otherwise, they just stare across the table at one another like *chiens de faience*."

A man in livery appeared with a plate of mushrooms marinated in butter and sage. Sylvia chose the biggest one, stabbed it with a toothpick, then in an almost apologetic gesture accepted a cocktail napkin with exaggerated reserve.

"Do you know how many children die from being disciplined? For innocent behavior like bed-wetting and crying?" Leon asked.

"I never bed-wet." Sylvia answered.

"I have a ten-year-old son," said Leon.

"And he bed-wets?" asked Sylvia. She scanned the room.

"He's very special," answered Leon.

She wondered if the child was mentally retarded. No, the correct term was *challenged*. Or was it *exceptional*? She was vexed. "And let me guess," Sylvia said. "You spare the rod and spoil the child." She didn't wait for him to comment. "What's his name?" she asked.

"It varies. At four he wanted to be called *Da* because it sounded like Daddy. At six he wanted to be called *John*. You know, at that age, they want to assimilate with their peers. It was important, his mother and I thought, that he be able to choose. Now he wants to be called Beelzebub, *Bubba* for short."

She smiled wanly. "You're kidding me, right?"

While Leon's looks appealed to Sylvia, he seemed too much the New Age, emancipated type, the type who kept anything by Robert Bly on his night table. She was drawn to a different kind of man; men who played rugby and could throw a left hook, men who owned and openly admitted a raw ferocity dictated by the y chromosome.

She first learned she liked *machismo in extremis* during her undergrad years. Fraternity life at Dartmouth boasted pledges that head-butt and ate light bulbs. She had witnessed Norman Mailer head-butt the football team's tight end in the basement of *Beta Theta Pi*.

She found the sensitive male, overly invested in his feminine side, more sexless than not. She respected him, but in the mammalian scheme of things, the slavishly virile turned her on.

"This is the great conundrum," she said to Leon.

"What is?"

"Women say they want a nurturing man in their lives, then target Johnny Rotten." She excused herself and walked towards the stairs in search of the powder room. She heard a baby's muffled cry.

Despite the much-anticipated arrival of his first child, Aldo had recently expressed his marital woes to Sylvia, complaining about his "bloodless marriage" to gorgeous wife Brigit.

But what, Sylvia thought, *was he expecting, when all she'd ever wanted from the union was a manor home (luxe track worked) in the right zip, and a Neiman's charge? And what was he expecting from the marriage when all he wanted was an arm-charm and a flaxen hair'd daughter he could show off like a* Lamborghini?

"Self-clone," he had demanded of his wife on their honeymoon.

Sylvia climbed the stairs slowly. Now that Aldo was in the throes of some existential malaise, some search for meaning in his life, why was he blaming the Nordic Wonder Wife he'd mistaken himself into thinking could make him happy, for the lack of life in his marriage?

"It's Brigit's fault," Aldo had told Sylvia over coffee.

"What is?"

"*Everything,*" he'd said.

She told Aldo Brigit's ice-queen agenda was probably a phase, "Unless she's a true Norwegian." She said, "Your marriage just needs a transfusion! A boost!"

"What should I do?" Aldo asked. "Buy a cock-ring?"

On the second floor she noticed the Chinese Oriental runners, pale as parchment. Where there was color it was muted. Some reds would have worked well, added drama. Interior decorating was like sex; it needed *frisson*. Brigit's use of neutrals had the numbing effect of Sodium Pentothal.

She wondered about the couple's sex life. Peeking into the master bedroom she recalled the scene in the movie, *Cat On A Hot Tin Roof,* where Burl Ives as Big Daddy points to the double bed in son-in-law Paul Newman's room and says, "When a marriage falls on the rocks the rocks lie here." Lack of sex was probably not ruining Aldo's marriage. It was most likely just the reverse. As far as Brigit's taste in decor went, it was insipid, but hardly conclusive evidence for a character smear. And really, when it came to Aldo's spousal disillusion, she reminded herself that men were political creatures. Truth was something they stretched.

She returned downstairs and found Leon at the bar.

"Tonic, please," he said to the bartender.

"I almost killed a deer getting here," he said to her.

"People should be fined for hitting animals," she said.

"You're kidding! What? Ten dollars for a squirrel? Fifty for a doe?"

"That's speciesism," Sylvia said.

"Tell me you're not one of those P.E.T.A. people," Leon said.

"I give them money. Let me guess. You're about to chew me out for wearing suede shoes."

"How tall are you in those heels?"

"Because if you were, I would tell you everything admits of degrees. Some P.E.T.A. sympathizers don't even wear cultured pearls! They somehow feel the oysters are exploited by being intentionally irritated with sand. I wear pearls."

"What about a thong. Do you wear a thong?"

"You're beginning to annoy me."

"Do you know the Roman Catholic take on animal rights?" Leon asked.

"I know stories," Sylvia answered. "Saint Francis preaching to the birds, Saint Giles rescuing deer, Saint Columba saving the crane. Just because they are stories, sentimental ones at that, doesn't mean they don't resonate theologically. These stories have moral themes."

Aldo put on a CD of R.E.M. Leon's head bobbed in sync.

"Saint Thomas Aquinas, in *Summa Contra Gentiles* wrote, 'By divine providence animals are intended for man's use in the natural order.'"

"The Dalai Llama," Sylvia responded, "condemns men killing animals for sport, pleasure, and adventure. He's even opposed to wearing fur. Calls it disgusting."

Leon stirred his drink with a swizzle stick.

"In Genesis," she continued, "an animal-free diet is commanded. And in Judaism, well, the Hebrew phrase *tsa'ar ba'alei chayim* is the biblical mandate to not cause pain to any living creature. Look, when it comes to the Catholic Church, your buddy Aquinas is not the consummate authority."

His voice was aspirant and on the high side, his stomach not the property of someone disciplined to exercise regularly. Her voice, on the other hand, was low. Telephone operators called her sir. She did one hundred sit-ups a day. Maybe they were more compatible than she thought.

"Fish, by the way, have highly developed central nervous systems," she said. "They feel pain. Do you fish?"

"Not to sound prosaic or anything, but why don't you worry about people?" Leon asked. "People have souls."

"Animals have rich cognitive experiences and, I believe, souls."

"You know, Aquinas—in *Summa Theologica*—says animals are not owed even kindness out of charity, that they share no fellowship with man in the rational life. He says charity doesn't extend to irrational creatures."

"Aquinas is a thirteenth-century jerk—I mean *he's* not, but that statement is inane. I mean, why then, don't we incinerate all the coma victims and severely brain-damaged children? They aren't rational! Anyway, whoever said loving God is a rational exercise?" She lowered her voice. "Look, more compassion and kindness belong to the weak and powerless. And as far as that rational thing goes, I know a poodle who does square roots!"

"Brigit's mother looks like a poodle," Leon volunteered, shifting his focus to the foyer and an older woman with tight curly hair and a long nose. "Aldo says she can be a real bitch."

"You say that like it's a *bad* thing." Sylvia laughed.

"Photo op!" A lithe redhead with a Polaroid sprang into view. "You two, move closer!"

Leon grabbed Sylvia's waist and drew her to him. She pictured the shot, how they would look together, their Mediterranean coloring, their substantial frames. But it was the pressure of his fingertips between her rib and hipbone that she would summon later. Alone in bed she would replay the tactile memory when she woke throughout the night.

For Christmas, she gave him a copy of *The Brothers Karamazov*, her favorite work by Dostoevsky marking with a sterling bookmark the page with Father Zossima's sermon to his monks, one of the most stirring sermons she'd ever read.

"Love all God's creation, the whole of it, and every grain of sand. Love every leaf, every ray of God's light…Love the animals: God has given them the rudiments of thought and untroubled joy. Do not, therefore, trouble it. Do not torture them. Do not deprive them of their joy. Do not go against God's intent. Man, do not exalt yourself above the animals: they are without sin, while you with your majesty defile the earth by your appearance on it. You leave traces of your defilement behind you—alas this is true of almost every one of us."

He gave her a bonsai tree, ironic considering her predilection for youth. Over the phone one evening she told him she typically had "a thing for younger men," men ten years her junior. "I used to punish myself for being attracted to them. Dating guys that young just didn't seem appropriate, but then I asked myself, what does 'appropriate' mean anyway? It's a word used to describe hostess gifts and stationery, a word used to describe the world of manners, not the world of the heart."

"You're telling me it's not a physical thing with these guys?"

"Of course it is! But it's more! Younger men are so full of energy, spilling over to please, so pure and impressionable."

"Young calves you can brand," Leon said.

"What an irresponsible analogy," she muttered.

They talked about heroin chic, mannequins with black and blue faces in department store windows. "Didn't they do this in the early eighties?" she asked. "I remember being in Manhattan and passing Barney's on Sixth Avenue, thinking, *My God, battered women have become* soigné. Then I noticed the mannequins breathing! They were lively! Luminous in these gauzy gowns. It was clearly a gender thing. I never saw bruised men floating around in Barney's windows."

They talked about some rakish fashion designer waltzing one of his models down the runway in a crown of thorns.

"Does an aesthetic of butchery really surprise you when partial-term abortions are being considered a legal option?" she asked.

"Abortion kills. And what is being killed is a living human being who, when aborted, has arms; legs, a brain, and a beating heart." She took a breath and continued. "What about the baby, now in his third trimester, delivered—all but his head—kicking and screaming while the doctor jams the scissors into the base of his skull! Sadly, the infinitely important, self-preoccupied feminists think this is about them."

They talked about art.

"De Kooning," Sylvia said, "in the fifties told some art critic, maybe Clement Greenberg, that it was impossible to paint a face. Why is it any easier now?"

"It's an anatomical fact," she reminded him days later, dabbing perfume behind her ears as he waited in her living room to take her to dinner. "Whether it's babies or animals. They have no developed cerebral cortex. They can't will harm. May I offer you a drink?" she asked in the next breath. "Some Perrier?"

"I'm set, thanks."

"Animals, like babies, are pure. And purity counts more than intelligence in the eyes of God." She straightened the seam in her black hose. "Most animals are saints. Not cruel for fun the way men and women are. They don't get off on that."

Leon appeared to change the subject, but was actually buttressing her observation about the sexes with a not-incongruous notion of his own. "Falling in love is like any other crisis. It gives you an opportunity to change."

She pulled a pair of elbow-length gloves from her drawer. "Why did you and your wife split?" she asked.

She adjusted her short skirt as she slid into his sedan. She was absolutely attracted to him and wondered when they would sleep together. *Better wait,* she thought, aware from experience of the damage done when sex preempted familiarity and trust earned in a relationship.

She noticed the key ring dangling from the ignition, some clay impressionist thing, the obvious work of a child. She wondered if his son provided him with the love he needed to operate, the love that made the quotidian bearable. She wondered if he over invested in the relationship to get the huge returns he needed.

"My ex-wife was a couch potato."

"You left your wife because she watched a lot of television?"

"She was also having affairs. I had no idea until one day one of her swains shows up at my door with a .45. It was the Mexican ambassador! Here this pint-sized Lothario, this pinto bean is screaming he will never go to jail for murder because he has diplomatic immunity!"

"What did you do?"

"What else? I invited him in for a drink!"

She tittered with glee. He stopped at a red light.

"You want to know the truth? Honestly? My wife didn't need me. A man needs to feel needed."

And the unconditional love from a child, Sylvia thought, *a child Leon happened to spoil silly, a child who made him feel indispensable, is addressing that need for him. What adult relationship could provide him that same luxury?*

"So when was the last time you were in love?" she asked.

"I lived with a twenty-year-old for a while. We recently broke up. She left a message on my machine a couple of weeks ago saying she can't live without me."

"A man told me that once, and you know what I said? 'If you can't live without me, then why aren't you dead yet?'"

The restaurant was chic, the *maitre d'hotel* obsequious, the clientele lacking, as is usual in the Nation's Capital, any veritable glamour. They ordered *risotto con funghi*. She passed on the raw *langostino* with coarse sea salt.

"I don't eat anything with a face."

"May I suggest the *Bresaola* celery root and baby green salad with truffle vinaigrette?" asked the waiter.

"Sounds good," she said.

"Two," Leon replied.

"And one martini for me," Sylvia said. "*Belvedere,* neat."
"So how adoring was this delicious sprite?" she asked.

Now she felt even more qualified to assume he needed to feel potent and revered, needed adoration and attention. She realized this was, in fact, her own emotional predicament. That those traits that offended us most in others, thrived robustly in ourselves.

"I mean, wouldn't you have been happier with someone more…" she hated the word, *mature,* "someone who brought a bit more, well, *symmetry* to the relationship?"

"Look who's talking, cradle robber!"

He broke off a piece of *focaccia.* "Apparently this girl is living in London with some sheik from Abu Dhabi. I feel sorry for her. She had borderline personality disorder and was bulimic. I never knew."

"Tell it to Oprah!"

"She was a college drop-out, a beer-fortune heiress, melancholic like those waif-like heroines in French movies."

Sylvia folded the linen napkin on her lap. "What draws you to contaminated relationships?" she asked. She loved that phrase, *contaminated relationship.*

"Have some compassion, Sylvia."

"For a trust-fund baby with every opportunity in the world? Leon, get real."

The waiter arrived with their meal.

"The funny thing is, she reminds me of you! She was privileged, sent to a private school in Switzerland, fluent in French and Italian, interested in art, actually quite talented as a photographer."

"Oh, please! So what happened?"

"I got tired of kissing her ass."

Sylvia thanked the waiter. The steam from Leon's asparagus lifted.

"Did Lolita have a *métier*? Or did she just suck the teat of her parents' bank account?"

"She was in college, for Chrissakes."

"Okay, all I'm saying is she sounds like she had emotional issues, and if you felt you needed to swoop down and save her from her own demise—well, that doesn't make you any sounder emotionally than she was. Haven't you heard the theory that people seek their own emotional quotient in a partner? If she was screwed up then you were too."

"You and I are together right now," Leon said. "Does that make us screwed up? If you're calling me an emotional cripple then welcome to the club."

"You've obviously wised up. Look, Leon, we're all flawed. I could have bought a townhouse with what I've spent on shrinks. But when it comes to compassion, I save mine for real victims: cancer patients, crack babies, the homeless, not some blonde nymphet who feels compelled to regurgitate her last bite of *crème brûlée* so she can squeeze into a size two."

She realized this tirade had cost her points with him, and once more, that any venom spilled for his young ex, her trappings, tastes, and shallow mercies, was just more self-chastisement.

"So tell me about your last young buck," Leon said.

"Strange that you should ask. His name was Buck."

"No!"

"He was twenty, not exactly MENSA material. He picked me up in the college library. He knew I was a professor. The boy had balls."

With affected languor, Leon stretched.

"He looked like a young Tony Curtis!" Sylvia continued. "Fabulous! Hairy! I could tell because the top buttons of his shirt were open."

"Tacky," Leon said.

"Why?"

Sylvia liked hairy men the way Japanese women liked Sean Connery in his dubbed 007 movies."Buck was advanced in a profound way. He had an uncanny sense of what it means to be alive."

"How so?"

"One tip-off was, he never rushed. Each moment was considered, not as a prelude to the next or footnote to the last. And he sang, he sang in his car, in elevators. He loved to sing. I think people who sing are a special lot. He couldn't even carry a tune, which made me so envious. I have perfect pitch and hate to sing!"

Leon leaned forward.

"He was studying to be a fireman, right? And well, he basically lived at the fire station where he slept on this ragged, burnt cot. One morning, as the sun was rising, he was summoned to rally. He's telling me this and begins to describe the color of the morning to me, and I'm a painter. I know color. But the way he's talking about it, and it wasn't just the actual words he used, not just the text, but *the subtext*, to borrow a thespian phrase. I mean I have steeped myself in art criticism and I'm familiar with how color is spoken about. But his account—it was unassailable!

"Then he arrives at this caddy shack and does CPR on this old man, reviving him. And through it all, he hears God calling. He recognizes a call to know God, to love Him and serve Him, which incidentally, was exactly what he was doing!"

"Are you saying he heard the voice of God?"

"Yes! He heard God calling his name. You mean audibly? Phonetically? I don't know. Maybe, maybe not. I don't think it matters. My point is, Little Tony Curtis might blow a standard I.Q. test, but his intuition, his sensitivity to the beauty and order of life, his strong moral imagination stunned me. What a turn on! I could not have enough sex with him after that."

"You certainly have a lot of sex for an unmarried Catholic," Leon said, and quickly added, "How's your *risotto*?"

A cloak of sadness fell over her face. She lifted her martini glass to her lips. She wanted to tell Leon she was sorry for having felt empty, sorry for her pride, her lust, her lack of self control, her neediness, her loneliness. She wanted to tell him that she, too, was a human being, and on balance not a bad person, maybe even a good person, but instead she sipped the cool vodka, filtered, she had heard somewhere, twenty-seven times. It tasted like water.

"Tony saw the sacred in the ordinary. He could see a flock of geese flying in V formation and drop to his knees as if he had experienced a miracle."

The waiter whisked by, then reappeared to clear the table.

"I asked Little Tony—he would freak if he heard me calling him Little Tony—he's 6 foot 4, 230 pounds—anyway, I asked him if he was interested in seeing a documentary on Nixon. Do you know what? He didn't even know Nixon had been a U.S. president!"

"C'mon!"

"Seriously. When we went out for morning coffee I would read the paper, and he would watch me reading the paper. If you want to know the truth that bugged the hell out of me. It's weird. What I like about younger men is their fresh read on things, and here this guy pisses on the freshest read around!"

"Literally?"

"You pervert! Of course not."

"Espresso?" asked the waiter.

"Would you care for coffee?" Leon asked her.

"Please," she answered.

"Two," Leon told the waiter.

"I take it Little Tony was quite the stud performer."

"He did have this terrific kinetic Intelligence. He danced like a Zulu, and I mean that in an ancient tribal sense. Dancing to communicate with the gods! Trying to become an angel by shaking off his genitals!"

She poured what was left of the bottled mineral water into her glass. "Once I took Little Tony…"

"Haven't you delighted us long enough with Little Tony tales?"

"Leon, I took the poor guy to an aerobics class, and he was lost! Even though he was agile, had perfect rhythm, not to mention amazing muscle memory, all those programmatic moves stymied him. He felt trapped."

She lit a Marlboro. The waiter arrived with their coffee and placed an anodyne ashtray in the center of the table.

"I can't understand a woman who takes care of herself the way you do and smokes. Reds, no less!"

"I think if I had someone to kiss every time I wanted to light up, I'd quit."

He reached under the table and grabbed her calf. With the other hand he motioned the waiter for the check.

"Don't put on your seatbelt," he said once they were inside the car. She obeyed. He pulled her to him in one swift move.

"Do I smell of smoke?" she asked.

"What do want me to say?" he answered.

"I'm surprised you're not one of those scent police. The rads who want to legislate scent federally," she said.

"Luv, you're the one who loves rules!"

"You're being facetious, right? If I had a problem with authority I wouldn't be a Catholic."

"You're a cafeteria Catholic. You pick and choose what rules suit you."

She rolled her window down a crack.

"You know my friend Rolando?" Leon asked. "Didn't you meet him at Aldo's? He owns his own Investment firm. He's Catholic. Very proud of subsidizing a Colombian orphanage. Personally took charge, this Christmas, of delivering a plane full of antibiotics to these orphans almost blown to bits from a nearby coca lab explosion. Would you believe this same Mr. Nice Guy has been banned from the Willard Dining Room because he spat at a waitress? He views servers as ciphers yet fancies himself a good Catholic."

"Treat those who serve, as kings, kings among men," Sylvia said.

"That plane full of antibiotics. Why does charity have to be so operatic?" asked Leon.

"Listen," he said. "Do you want me to take you home? Are you tired? We could go somewhere for a nightcap. If you're up for it."

"Sure, I'm up for it."

"Sullivan's okay?"

"Fine."

He made a wide U turn.

"You know," Sylvia began, "people bash Mother Teresa, say she is spoiling the poor, robbing them of their dignity by giving them handouts, freebies, and do you know what she says? She says God spoils us. 'Look at all the free things He has given us. We breathe and don't pay for oxygen! What would happen,' she asks, 'if God were to say, "Work for one hour and you'll get sunshine for two!" How many of us would survive?'"

He reached across the seat for her hand.

"I have a question for you," she said. "Actually I wanted to ask it when we met, and you told me you covered wars. I want to know how you handled it? How did it *not* do a number on you? Did you figure out a way to anesthetize yourself?"

"Who said I handled it?" Leon asked. "Who said war didn't do a number on me? I'll tell you one thing. That entire experience made me stop drinking!"

He paused and looked out at the sky, a furnace of light.

"Most people drink to numb pain, to blur reality," he continued. "Just the reverse of what would happen to me when I drank. My drinking brought the pain front and center. Clarified it. Drinking sharpened the reality."

"Isn't that what psychotherapy is supposed to do?" she asked.

"Force a person to confront his pain?" he answered.

"It's more like *invite* a person to confront his pain," she replied.

Leon did not want to talk about psychotherapy. "I think this whole anti-alcohol movement, this abstemious, pious trend is a joke," he began. "Remember when people drank liquor? Now it's just beer and wine, and if you're lucky your host may have *white* liquor in his cabinet. The cocktail is dead."

"Drinking alcohol is an ancient, venerated social tradition, practiced often in sacred ritual," Sylvia said.

"You crack me up," Leon countered. "The tone you just used! You sounded like a Jeopardy contestant. Listen, I *stopped* drinking to numb the effect these African wars had on me. How did I dwarf feeling the full impact of that powerful experience? *By sobering up!*"

"Leon, would you mind if we skipped Sullivan's? I'm suddenly beat."

"No problem. It's a good thirty minutes to your house anyway."

Sylvia began talking about a girlfriend of hers they'd bumped into at the movies two weeks before. "She's dating some sleaze-ball who's after her job. Caught him schmoozing her boss last week."

"So he's done," Leon said.

"Not really. Sondra swears worthy adversaries make the best lovers."

Leon had caught the proverbial bee in his bonnet. "Sylvia, don't you see the significance? Jesus changing water into wine? You know, the wine used in most Christian liturgies *symbolizes* the blood of Christ. But the wine used in Catholic Masses, through *transubstantiation*, actually *becomes* the blood of Christ."

It began to rain heavily. Bolts of moisture hit the window like small stones. Leon pulled the car over. His focus shifted from the handbrake to the flashers.

"I think my drinking was a means I used to get closer to God," Leon said. He turned the windshield wipers off.

"Why do you think Carl Jung waited until he was eighty-six, ready to croak, to express an opinion he held holy but feared would be misconstrued?" Leon asked. "He said his friend's 'craving for alcohol, was the equivalent, on a low level, of our spiritual thirst for wholeness'—and then Jung quotes scripture: 'As the heart panted after the water brooks, so panted my soul after thee, O God.' Jung noted that the word 'alcohol,' *spiritus* in Latin, defines the highest religious experience."

He turned the heat up in the car. She stared at the floor mats.

"Why didn't you tell me you had won a Pulitzer?"

"Sylvia, I'm a reporter. I appear on the scene, observe, and ask questions a smart thirteen-year-old would—then—connect the dots."

"But your talent to tell the story, move people, move them to act, to right wrongs—"

"I often wonder if my readers get It. I'm not being condescending here; really I'm not. But I've seen Congolese babies lofted for bayonet practice. I mean, please, how many ordinary U.S. citizens can relate to that?"

"Why would you write about it if you thought they couldn't? What would be the point?"

"You think *The Washington Post's* affluent readers, snug in their tax shelters and Bass Weejuns, can understand the plight of the truly disconsolate? Reminds me of those preachers in their Silver Clouds extolling the virtues of poverty. They're not getting it either."

The rain, a medley of drums, continued to beat on the car.

"And you, Sylvia? How do you reconcile your faith and its great respect for the poor with your greater respect for the monied? An exclusionary agenda is not exactly a Christ-infused M.O."

"The awful news is that a million bucks a year makes you middle class on Park Avenue these days," she said, trying to lighten up the conversation.

Leon chuckled. "I remember dating this girl," he said, "years ago. She'd graduated with honors from Cornell, and then moved to Manhattan to work for *W*, the gossip magazine, filled with photos of the *demi monde*. She dressed the part, Yves Saint Laurent, Kenzo. Ruthlessly beautiful! Looked like one of Botticelli's putti: porcelain skin, golden curls. She knew things! Knew a fugue when she heard one, knew supply-side economics, knew how to make tiramisu. Yeah, she was one of the *hipoisie*, the *cognoscenti*, and guess what? Like Eva Peron, she hated the rich! She hated the people who owned and operated the magazine! She hated the people who read the magazine! Not necessarily the people but their values. So I asked her, how can you spend fifty hours a week working for this glossy? Why don't you write for *The Free Press*? Why are you writing about Bulgari jewelry when you could be exposing slum lords in the Bronx?"

"And what did she say?"

"What could she say? She had never been in a slum in her life! And, are you ready for this? She wore Bulgari jewelry!"

"What a hypocrite!"

"We're all hypocrites, Sylvia! Isn't it true that all these people we anathematize may also live complex, contradictory lives? Don't we?"

"Of course we do. But I don't feel comfortable cutting myself any slack for it. The way I see it, self-compassion has the uncompromising ability to bleed into personal lassitude, something I find grotesque."

"Let's motor," he said. He put the key in the ignition and started the engine.

"You know the old boyfriend who told me he couldn't live without me?" Sylvia asked. "Did I mention whenever he got into a tizzy he exuded an odor? Like a musk ox! He was physically intimidating."

"You loved it!"

"What a troll!"

He opened her door and helped her out of the car. The air was cool and moist. The trees on the street looked like large women in veils.

"Don't you think, Sylvia, that if there were something immoral about eating fish, God wouldn't have multiplied two to feed five thousand hungry people?"

"The Bible is poetry."

"So the miracle of the five loaves and two fish didn't happen?"

"Maybe the miracle involved just the bread. Maybe Christians added fish to the story later for symbolic purposes. Who knows? So they ate fish back then. Can't we credit ourselves with evolving? Didn't Paul somewhere in Corinthians advocate slavery?"

They took their time walking on the broken stone path leading to her red front door.

"I want you to meet my son," Leon said.

She reached in her jacket pocket for her key. "When?" Sylvia asked.

"Tomorrow?" he whispered.

She hugged him and buried her head in the fleece lining of his coat.

On her way to Leon's the next morning, she stopped for coffee at a convenience mart. Their blend tasted better than what she found in the boutique beaneries. Near the checkout line she grabbed a two-foot green plastic Aquaman equipped with scuba gear and Infrared goggles. She gave the clerk a twenty, and didn't bother to count the change. Driving, she studied the sky's tone. Pewter, hemmed in blue. She remembered a studio art teacher who'd memorized three hundred shades of blue. She probably did a lot of L.S.D., Sylvia thought.

Leon answered the door in bare feet. "Welcome," he said. He pulled her towards him and bit her playfully on the lips. "C'mon in," he added, leading her into his rustic home. The fire was lit. A Sonny Rollins CD was playing.

"Bubba is hiding," he said.

She followed Leon into the boy's bedroom where Bubba popped out of the closet, screaming. The child was lanky, with buck teeth. A mole, shaped, she decided, like a pentagram, grew between the forest of his brows. *Hilarious,* she thought.

"Whoa, whoa," Leon tried to restrain Bubba who now was laughing and trying to get away.

"Bubba, I'd like you to meet Sylvia."

Bubba stared at her. "You said she was pretty! She's uglee-e-e-!" He spun around until he lost his balance and fell.

"Dude," she said, "I've got something for you." She reached into her Fendi tote and produced Aquaman, wrapped in a nautical map. He snatched it from her hand, ripped the paper, threw the plastic figure on the floor and ran out of the room. Leon gave her an all-at-once sympathetic and embarrassed smile. She picked up Aquaman, now broken, walked over to the large aquarium on the oak credenza, and gently dropped him in. She stood, for several minutes, hypnotized by the ballet of exotic fish.

Sublime, she thought. *Wasn't it Plotonius who said, "The soul that beholds beauty becomes beautiful"?*

Bubba re-appeared and banged on the aquarium glass with his knuckles. She ignored him. He banged harder.

"Bubba!" his father called. The boy ran toward him and strapped his gangly arms around his father's trunk.

"Video store, video store video store, video store, video store!" he shouted.

"I promised Bubba we'd rent a movie," Leon said.

"We?"

"He doesn't like to watch movies alone."

"Gulliver's Travels is a fun movie," said Sylvia.

"Fuck Gulliver!" Bubba squealed and then collapsed into a pile of dirty clothes stacked outside his room.

Her gaze wandered back to the aquarium. She watched the membranous fin curtains of the black mollies undulate like perfect sine waves. She recalled the teleological argument for God's existence, the argument from nature, from design. She looked at the magnificent tints of the neon tetras, their gleaming skins.

She remembered when she was eight and her father had forced her to go fishing, insisting it would be good for her, "a new experience." She remembered the struggling fish hoisted on deck, their mouths bloodied from the hooks in their cheeks. She remembered their silver bodies lurching on the boat's deck in a halting effort to stay alive.

"They can't breathe!" she'd cried. She became horrified as the numbers grew. Some fish were big. A friend of her father's took a picture of a crew member holding up a dying fish.

"Smile!" the photographer said, snapping the shutter. She ran into a cabin and hid in a storage closet. "Get back on deck," her father had ordered. She obeyed and watched in terror as they scaled the fish with knives.

After they had gone to the video store, they stopped for ice cream. "My treat," Sylvia said. Bubba ordered a butterscotch sundae, took two bites, and then complained of stomach pains.

Sylvia turned to Bubba and said, "Boys your age in Addis Ababa eat sand. Do you know why?"

"I know what a blow job is," Bubba answered.

"That's enough," Leon said.

"They eat sand because their stomachs pain. They are starving," Sylvia said.

"Liar, liar, pants on fire!" Bubba chanted.

Bubba motioned to Sylvia to bend down. "My father likes his hooter sucked," he whispered in her ear.

Bubba steered the car home while Leon managed the brake and gas pedal. They missed the rear fender of a Lincoln Town Car by a hair.

"Dumb bitch," Bubba called the driver.

"You're listening to too much rap music," Leon said.

"Gonna make the bitch eat sand," Bubba replied.

Once home, inside of fifteen minutes, Leon and Bubba decided to go for a hike. They'd asked Sylvia to join them, but she passed, preferring to nap on the chenille sofa in front of the fireplace. When she woke up she looked at the clock on the mantel. She'd slept for fifty minutes.

"Leon?" she called. She peered out the bay window and observed a sky splintered with light. "Leon?" She wanted a cigarette, knew she had a pack in the glove compartment of her car. She folded the knitted throw she'd used to cover herself and walked to the carport. She hadn't locked the car. The door on the driver's side was ajar. Like an animal, she smelled harm.

Strewn on the passenger seat were the aquarium fish; the neon tetras, the elegant zebras, their bodies bent in vulgar arcs, the collapsed guppies, their mouths open, their hearts visible through their thin skin.

She crouched on the cold cement, her head lowered, cradled in her hands. Eyes shut, she tried to block the scene from her mind but couldn't, compelled by some strange desire to replay it. As if it were almost the price for being alive. She remembered a line from Faulkner. "Between grief and nothingness I'll take grief." It seemed to her these days even the earth was grieving, her ravines filled with radium and nuclear waste, her seas rife with sewage, her poisoned fish, like sins, darkening the once-white beaches. She grieved in kind, in sympathetic resonance., like a dog that hears a horn and howls to mimic it.

Bubba had meant to hurt her. Uncanny that he'd pulled a scene from her childhood he could so easily re-dramatize. Violation of the Innocents. She felt called to their plight. She was not sure this was not a noble calling. Relentlessly, the scene reappeared in her mind's eye. Again she tried to control it, imagining her brain a blank square with black borders, impermeable to invasion. But the scene of the kill still managed to push through, brazenly, this time, as if it were aware of its own exacting permanence.

She thought of Michelangelo sculpting. He said the image was always there; he just chipped away at the marble around it. It had been too long since she had picked up a paintbrush.

She herself longed for a kind of permanence, a continuity of sorts. But in what arena? Her personal life? A partner? A child? Her art? Her eclipsed commitment to painting was manageable precisely because she could and did snake out of it when the pressure was on.

Paint the carport fish kill scene? Maybe Bubba was the catalyst to jumpstart her career again. She remembered a not-dumb old boyfriend once saying she had a genius for *feeling*, not *painting*, that her real talent was for *life*, not *art*.

"Bullshit," she'd said and never returned his calls after that. She was good. She reminded herself of the gallery shows maxed to capacity at a time when she was too young to appreciate it, the famous agent (who handled the brightest stars on the Slavic-art front) courting her for months to sign with him.

Still somehow she felt her painting didn't move people the way Leon's writing did. He could tell the tragic tale; she couldn't. Which is why she stopped painting, and he won citations. Yet she felt everything, and he felt nothing. An occupational hazard he had wantonly admitted to, a self-induced numbness he'd coveted to preserve the self.

"What kind of a masochist are you anyway?" he'd asked her once over breakfast.

She looked at the spill of bodies, bits of jeweled flesh splayed on black vinyl. She looked at the angelfish, its torn fin pierced by a file of light. She remembered the letters of the Greek word for *fish* (*ICHTHYS*). She remembered they formed an acrostic of the words *Jesus Christ, Son of God*. She bowed her head, and with an inviolable need, called her Savior by name.

She cabbed it home where she found a message from Leon on her answering machine.
"Sylvia, It's Leon. I've cleaned your car. I'd like to drive it over. I'm dropping Bubba at his mother's. I am sorry, really I am."
She picked up the phone and dialed him. What was she doing with this jaded infidel and his vile son, who'd probably grow up to be the next Richard Speck? Leon and his ex-wife shared custody, so the boy wasn't going anywhere soon.
She thought she might be falling in love with Leon. But so what? Falling in love was a walk in the park. Idiots did it all the time. The pivotal question was why would she want an emotionally stunted man? A man who'd told her he'd spent all the love he had. A man who jokingly referred to himself as *damaged goods*. Weren't jokes masks for truths?

The line was busy. She pressed redial.
Their world views clashed. He wasn't even her physical type. She spied a Marlboro pack under a sheaf of papers.
If this relationship was good why was she feeling bad?
"Hello," Leon said, sotto voce.

"A woman without a man cannot meet a man, any man, any age, without thinking, even if it's for a half-second, Perhaps this is the man." —Doris Lessing

January 1997
Leon and Sylvia
Washington, D.C.

"If I were the devil and I really wanted to punish you, I would give you great success in something you didn't believe in." In a red camisole, facing him in her bed, she added, "But then you don't believe in the devil, do you?"

"I'd rather fail at something I love than succeed at something I hate," Leon replied.

She lightly ran her sharp fingernails across his chest. "Your nose just grew three inches, Pinocchio! You hate to fail, my sweet, virile incubus! Another testimony to your swollen ego."

"Lift up your nightgown."

With one thrust of her head, she let her mane of thick blonde hair sweep over his torso. "You think you've failed at love," she said.

"You know one of the definitions of insanity?" he answered. "Repeating the same effort, over and over, expecting different results." In the next breath he added, "And, babe, I do believe in the devil! Look at my ex-wife! And a few of the women I've dated! They might as well cleave with goats!"

"What does that say about you?" Sylvia gently poked him in the ribs.

"Women!" he bellowed. "Proud of this metaphysical power they imagine they posses. Power to change a man! Talk about ego! Women need to know: Men Don't Change!"

"And what calculus of influence…" she began.

"Pride," he waxed on, "once the devil's *porte cochere*, has become…"

"Leon!" she interrupted. "How can you be such a jerk and so fabulous too?" She tongued his lips, running the nails of her other hand along the high inside of his roped thighs.

Two mornings ago he'd told her he was leaving for Rwanda, that he had been re-assigned to write a companion series for dispatches he'd begun for *The Washington Post* in 1994. Now, after dating her over a month, he informed her he didn't know when he would see her again.

"Did you know Robert Mitchum was a truck driver from Rising Sun?" she asked.

"Do you know Larry, the gynecologist you met at Aldo's? His girlfriend stays with him in the hospital when he's on call. Apparently he has access to liquid cocaine. They rub it over their genitals and copulate all night until he gets paged to deliver a baby, which he attempts with a 45-degree erection."

"I never met Larry. I met his wife. She would love that story."

Leon shifted his focus to a crack in the wall, a fine crack in the plaster from which others would follow. So he figured happened with a man's character. Precisely what Leon feared for himself. His subtle and perfect demise, so fine, so painstakingly gradual, almost imperceptible. One of these days he would wake up a moral eunuch.

"Okay, what's your idea of a metaphorical hell on earth?" he asked.

"Living a lie," she answered, "Waking up every day, so far away from who you really are. That's hell."

Suddenly, she felt his whole body contract, a chill prevail.

"You don't know what happened," he said.

"Tell me what happened. Tell me your secret sin," she chided, ignorant of what was to come. What was to come was more than she cared to know.

Leon sat upright in bed and looked at her without blinking. For a long while—was it ten minutes, was it?—he didn't move. His eyes glazed, fixing on a point not past her but through her. Then, lapsing into a kind of trance he began a recitation. Almost chant like. For fifty minutes he sustained the litany of facts. *Fifty minutes, the length of a Roman Catholic Mass. Fifty minutes, the length of a psychoanalytic session, a considered confession and absolution.*

He wept. His head hung like a pale moon in the swamp of her chest. He talked. Talking, he shed light on the situation. She listened, rapt and repelled.

He: "In Nyarubuye."
She: "Where?"
He: "A remote village in the high savannah of southeast Rwanda called *The Place of Stones.*"
She: "Go on."
He: "A Roman Catholic parish."
Sylvia's eyes narrowed.
He: "She was a Tutsi, stock-still among a scrum of corpses. Hutu butchers. In 4 days they killed 1000 of her clan. In 100 days, they killed 850,000. Bullets blazed through the banana trees. She was maimed under a blue sky. Fending off ax blows to her head. She lost her hand.

"Her attackers left her for dead. She lay crumpled, like a paper bag, next to her dead mother."

"Sit up," Sylvia said.

He: "Maria lay next to a large stone Hutus used to sharpen blades—dulled from cutting bones, white bones of the dusk-dazed. Every story centers on a quest and ends with a sacrifice.

"You think I'm being clever? The grounds of God became the killing grounds," he said, his voice flat like pummeled clay. "She was alive under the rubble of bodies. At night, bands of wild dogs came to feed on the dead. Too weak to stand, she threw stones to scare the dogs. Her parents were killed in front of her."

"You are sweating," Sylvia said to Leon.

He: "A fog hung in rags beneath the trees. The killers worked eight-hour shifts. At night they went home to their families. 'Tiring work,' one said, 'cutting open pregnant women. Exhausting.'"

"Here, have some water." Sylvia handed him a glass from the nightstand.

Leon drank, then spoke, as if by rote: "April 1994. 1000 Tutsis, fled to Nyarubuye, to this Catholic Church for Mass. Hutu extremists had just seized power in Rwanda. Their aim: kill all Tutsis. In 100 days over 850,000 people would be slaughtered. The radio this Sunday morning was the great battery-operated cheerleader! A mob surrounded the big transistor as if it were a cow, giving milk to the masses. 'We will kill them slowly, slowly, slowly.' The killers herded their victims into church. Children's heads were smacked together like cymbals. The radio reminded the Hutus of Colonial days when Tutsi chiefs were feudal overlords. Hutus cried, 'Don't let those cockroaches make slaves of you!' Across Rwanda, the slaughter was being repeated. No Tutsi was safe.

"Maria is the secret I carry with me," Leon said.

He began to shake violently, as the winter sun bled into the room, and he cried, fiercely, like a drinker deprived of his solace.

Sylvia recalled reading about Rwanda in the papers. She'd briefed herself by going back more than three decades to when Belgians who used the Tutsi minority to enforce their rules-ruled Rwanda. The Tutsis were the Rwandan aristocracy. The Hutu majority were farmers, a servile underclass. The dichotomy bred resentment, which erupted into violence as Belgians prepared to leave Rwanda in the late 1950s. In 1961, when Rwanda became independent, tens of thousands of Tutsis were forced from their homeland. In purge after purge, members of the Tutsi minority fled to Uganda where they formed The Rwandan Patriotic Front, a highly disciplined guerrilla army. In 1990 the Patriotic Front invaded Rwanda, determined to force the Hutu government to share power with the Tutsi minority. By the end of 1993, Rwanda's president, Habyarimana, caved in to pressure for talks. The Hutus thought their

President spineless, too ready to jettison the core of government of Hutu power. Extremists Hutus rigged an airplane carrying him and blamed the Tutsis for his death. As far as the Hutus were concerned, their leader had outlived his usefulness. Within hours of the plane crash, the genocide began.

Sylvia held Leon tightly. She wanted to comfort him. She kissed his forehead, his eyes, his cheeks, his salty lips. Tenderness at times came easily to her, a perennial surprise given her stern inclination for so many people and things.

His body glistened like a fish. Taut, wet, he glided inside her. She took the sea between her legs. The air, and soil, too. For it was not just him she wanted to connect with, but all creatures, finned and not, scrambling for life in this blighted world. She pressed her face against his. His cheekbones felt like stones covered with earth.

"I left Rwanda one night while Maria, pregnant with my child, slept on a cot in the church. I'd spent a week with her. I had not told her when I was leaving, if I would ever come back. She was sleeping the sleep of the seraphs."

Sylvia turned away from him, hiding sentiments that vexed her. She remembered a quote by Adrienne Rich, "A thinking woman sleeps with monsters. The beak that grips her she becomes." *But he wasn't a monster; monsters lacked conscience.* Hadn't he told her it was about faith? Faith he'd begun to lose in Liberia and by Rwanda had disappeared completely. Not only faith in God but faith in everything that lived and breathed and had its being.

"Why are you religious?" Leon asked her once.

"Just lucky, I guess," she answered.

"Not really," he replied, "just pressed, pressed for a context for feelings you don't understand."

In bed, the next morning, Sylvia thought, *How could he have abandoned a maimed girl, pregnant with his child, sleeping on a cot inside the church where her parents were murdered?* She desperately wanted to make sense of his actions. *Maybe,* she thought, *being a great craftsman, a marvelous technician, allowed him to write the tragedy without living it. Living it wasn't worth the pain. So he managed to avoid the real tragedy, the tragedy that fills every minute, the tragedy of what it means to be alive.* She felt a laser-like anguish for him. She peered outside the bedroom window. The clouds looked like wounds on the skin of the sky.

She recalled Leon's account from the night before.

Injured Maria, wary her attackers would return, lay motionless among the corpses. Much of Rwanda was decimated. The Tutsi guerrillas who'd formed the patriotic front now abandoned their cease-fire and penetrated Rwanda to try and save the Tutsis from extinction.

The Hutu refugees fled their advance. In twenty-four hours, a quarter of a million Hutus from eastern Rwanda crossed into Tanzania, the largest mass exodus of any people since World War II.

"Not a sparrow falls from a nest without God's approval," Sylvia had said. Leon's eyes flashed like armor as if he were angry at a comment he found almost viciously naive.

"I came with the Tutsi guerrillas to Nyarubuye and found Maria," he said. "She was dying. Looked like someone had scooped the flesh out from under her eyes with a teaspoon. Her machete wounds had festered for weeks."

Sylvia drew a deep breath.

"Some Tutsi soldiers and I took her to a makeshift clinic—no painkillers or antibiotics—she didn't cry—her face was—" he exhaled, "Her eyes were magnets."

Sylvia grabbed his wrists and pressed his pulse points to her mouth.

"I took this assignment to go back to Rwanda to find Maria. She's eighteen now. She was fifteen then. My daughter will be almost three."

"How do you know you have a daughter and not a son?"
"News travels," he said.
She said, "I don't think we can't love each other."

He stared at her balefully.
The next day Leon made preparations to leave the country.

PART TWO
NYARUBUYE

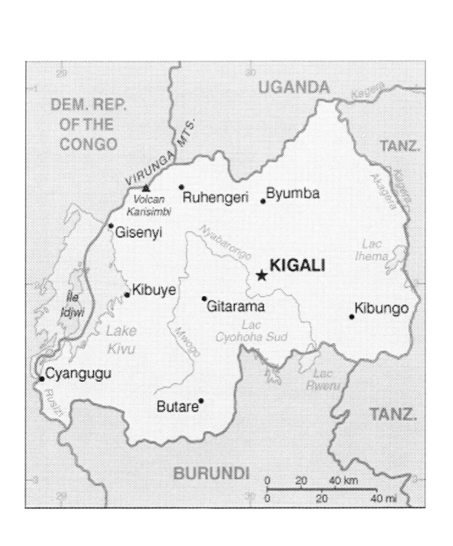

February 1997
Leon and Maria/Noel
Rwanda

He found Maria in the Nyrabuyan church where Hutus had killed her family three years earlier. She was kneeling on a *prie-dieu*, staring at a worn wooden and wire crucifix suspended from the ceiling. She didn't hear him enter. He came up behind her noiselessly and touched her shoulder. She flinched and turned around. A small smile influenced her lips. He looked in her eyes, the color of wine.

"I knew you would return," she said.

"How did you know?"

"How do you know when you have to sleep or eat or when you are thirsty?"

Through the open window, a bass line of Congo-Zaire rock was faintly audible.

"Because we have a daughter. You knew that. Did you know that?" she said.

Maria was beautiful, the shape of her head, the aquiline nose, the full lips with their perfectly angled philtrum. She was thin, a stalk of bark. Even her severed hand, cut with a *panga* blade, was, to him, beautiful. It told of suffering, and there was beauty in suffering if one was worthy of it, if one could dignify it. He stared at the wooden crucifix, the metal Christ made from electrical wire. He held her as the sound of distant gunfire spliced the afternoon.

"Her name is Noel. Leon spelled backwards. She is two years old. She was born on Christmas Day."

Maria needs me, Leon thought. *A man needs to feel needed, a woman, admired. Was this distinction accurate? Mercilessly facile? Moronic?*

Her hair smelled of sweet oil. Through the cotton shift she wore, he could feel her ribs. "Let's go get a beer," he said, "a good banana beer."

Inside the makeshift café they spoke. It had been almost three years since they had spent their one week together. Seated at a chipped metal table, Maria informed him of her daily life. She was a part-time teacher's aide at the local Catholic school. She was living with her aunt. She was uneasy about the Hutus, now living in her village, who had returned from the recently closed refugee camps in Zaire and Tanzania. The same men who had murdered her family and friends were her neighbors. She recognized them.

"Everyone is nervous," Maria began. "It's Rwanda's new Tutsi government's idea, settling the Hutus in their old villages, desegregating us, but Hutus are still killing. They show no remorse. Just a few months ago, *Interhamwe*, Hutu militia, marched into Nyrabuye, defiant and cold, past the skulls and bones. 'We are not done with the *inyenzi*, the cockroaches,' I heard one say. He wore a frayed bandana. His eyes were red from liquor. He had scabs on his legs."

She adjusted the strap of her white undershirt.

"I did not think my body would ever be strong enough to have a baby. How thin I was! 'Bones, all bones, jutting out like thieves,' you said. What did you mean—'bones like thieves'?"

"Bones taking over your dark-rum skin, robbing you of your beauty." He reached over the table and touched her hand, what was left.

"She looks like you," Maria said. "Certain expressions. Odd, she's never seen you make those expressions. She was born tiny, the size of a pop bottle. Seven months. Her skin is the color of your skin. Lighter than Tutsi skin."

She drank her Pepsi. He drank his beer. Leon wondered what had happened to her since he'd left Rwanda. After seeing her mother and father, neighbors, babies, axed to death. He looked at the scarred butt of her hand, her scarred face.

The proprietor, a lady in a yellow caftan stained under the arms, brought them dried sardines and some crackers.

On April 6th 1994, a jet carrying Rwanda's president, Juvenal Habyarimana, an alleged Hutu sympathizer, was shot down as it attempted to land near his palace in Kigali. Hutu extremists, unhappy with the president's consent to peace accords, were immediately suspected. Within an hour the mass slaughter began. A hundred-day orgy of murder would leave, by some estimates, as many as a million dead. What presaged and directly followed this seminal incident is condensed by Fergal Keane in *A Chronology of Genocide*, reprinted here as a reference.

A Chronology of Genocide

1918: Under the Treaty of Versailles, the former German colony of Rwanda-Urundi is made a UN protectorate to be governed by Belgium, adding to the vast Belgian possessions in the Congo. The two territories (later to become Rwanda and Burundi) are administered separately under two different Tutsi monarchs.

1926: Belgians introduce a system of ethnic identity cards differentiating Hutus from Tutsis.

1933: The colonial authorities carry out a census of the Rwandan population. Mandatory identity cards stating the ethnic identity of the bearer are extended.

1957: PARMEHUTU (Party for the Emancipation of the Hutus) is formed while Rwanda is still under Belgian rule.

1959: The Tutsi king, Mwaami Rudahigwa, dies. Hutus rise up against the Tutsi nobility and kill thousands. Many more flee to Uganda, Tanzania, Burundi, and Zaire.

1962: Rwanda gains independence from Belgium. Wide scale killing of Tutsis and further massive outflow of refugees, many to Uganda. Hutu nationalist government of Gregoire Kayibanda's PARMEHUTU comes to power.

1963: Further massacres of Tutsis, this time in response to military attack by exiled Tutsis in Burundi. Again more refugees leave the country. It is estimated that by the mid 1960s half of the Tutsi population is living outside Rwanda.

1967: Renewed massacres of Tutsis.

1973: Purge of Tutsis from university. Fresh outbreak of killings, again directed at Tutsi community. The chief of staff of the army, General Juvenal Habyarimana, seizes power, pledging to restore order. He sets up a one-party state. A policy of ethnic quotas is entrenched in all public service and military jobs. Tutsis are restricted to 9 percent of available jobs.

1975: Habyarimana's political party, the National Revolutionary Movement for Development (Mouvement Revolutionnaire National pour le Development or MRND) is formed. Hutus from the president's home area of northern Rwanda are given overwhelming preference in public service and military jobs. This pattern and the exclusion of the Tutsis continue throughout the seventies and eighties.

1986: In Uganda, Rwandan exiles are among the victorious troops of Yoweri Museveni's National Resistance Army who take power, overthrowing the dictator Milton Obote. The exiles form the Rwandan Patriotic Front (RPF), a Tutsi-dominated organization.

1989: The coffee price collapses, causing severe economic hardship in Rwanda.

July 1990: Under pressure from western aid donors Habyarimana concedes the principle of multi-party democracy.

October 1990: Tutsi guerrillas of the recently formed RPF invade Rwanda from Uganda. After fierce fighting in which French and Zairean troops are called in to assist the government, a cease-fire is signed on 29 March 1991.

1990/1991: The Rwandan army begins to train and arm civilian militias known as *Interhamwe* (those who stand together). For the next three years Habyarimana stalls on the establishment of a genuine multi-party system with power sharing.

Throughout this period thousands of Tutsis are killed in separate massacres around the country. Opposition politicians and newspapers are persecuted.

November 1992: Prominent Hutu activist Dr. Leon Mugusera appeals to Hutus to send the Tutsis back to Ethiopia via the rivers.

February 1993: the RPF launches a fresh offensive. The guerrillas reach the outskirts of Kigali and French forces are again called in to help the government side. Fighting continues for several months.

August 1993: At Arusha in Tanzania, following months of negotiations, Habyarimana agrees to power-sharing with the Hutu opposition and the RPF. He also agrees to integrate the RPF into a new Rwandan army, giving the guerrillas almost half the positions among officers and men. The presidential guard is to be merged with elite RPF troops into a smaller republican guard. 2,500 UN troops are subsequently deployed in Kigali to oversee the implementation of the accord.

September 1993 to March 1994: President Habyarimana stalls on setting up power-sharing government. Training of Hutu militia intensifies. Extremist radio station, Radio Mille Collines, begins broadcasting exhortations to attack the Tutsis. Human rights groups warn the international community of impending calamity.

March 1994: Many Rwandan human rights activists evacuate their families from Kigali, believing massacres are imminent.

6 April 1994: President Habyarimana and the president of Burundi, Cyprien Ntaryamira, are killed when Habyarimana's plane is shot down as it tries to land at Kigali Airport. Extremists, suspecting the president is finally about to implement the Arusha Peace Accords, are believed to be behind the attack. That night the killings begin.

7 April 1994: The Rwandan armed forces and the *Interhamwe* set up roadblocks and go from house to house killing Tutsis and moderate Hutu politicians. Thousands die on the first day. UN forces stand by while the slaughter goes on. They are forbidden to intervene, as this would breach their *monitoring* mandate.

8 April 1994: The RPF launches a major offensive to end the genocide and rescue 600 of its troops surrounded in Kigali. The troops had been based in the city as part of the Arusha Accords.

21 April 1994: The UN cuts the level of its forces from 2,500 to 250 following the murder of ten Belgian soldiers assigned to guard the moderate Hutu prime minister, Agathe Uwiliyingimana. The prime minister is killed, and the Belgians are disarmed, tortured, shot and hacked to death. They had been told not to resist violently by the UN force commander, as this would have breached their mandate.

30 April 1994: The UN Security Council spends eight hours discussing the Rwandan crisis. The resolution condemning the

killing omits the word "genocide." Had the term been used, the UN would have been legally obliged to act to "prevent and punish" the perpetrators. Meanwhile, tens of thousands of refugees flee into Tanzania, Burundi and Zaire. In one day 250,000 Rwandans, mainly Hutus fleeing the advance of the RPF, cross the border into Tanzania.

17 May 1994: As the slaughter of the Tutsis continues, the UN finally agrees to send 6,800 troops and policemen to Rwanda with powers to defend civilians. A fresh Security Council resolution says, "Acts of genocide may have been committed." The United States government forbids its spokespersons to use the word "genocide." Deployment of the mainly African UN forces is delayed because of arguments over who will pay the bill and provide the equipment. The United States argues with the UN over the cost of providing heavy armored vehicles for the peacekeeping forces.

22 June 1994: With still no sign of UN deployment, the Security Council authorizes the deployment of French forces in southwest Rwanda. They create a "safe area" in territory controlled by the government. Killings of Tutsis continue in the "safe area," although the French protects some. The United States government eventually uses the word "genocide."

July 1994: The final defeat of the Rwandan army. The government flees to Zaire, followed by a human tide of refugees. The French end their mission and are replaced by Ethiopian UN troops. The RPF sets up an interim government of national unity in Kigali. A cholera epidemic sweeps the refugee camps in Zaire, killing thousands. Different UN agencies clash over reports that RPF troops have carried out a series of reprisal killings in Rwanda. Several hundred civilians are said to have been executed. Meanwhile the killing of Tutsis continues in refugee camps.

Now almost three years later, Leon had made a decision to find Maria. A woman he'd met in Washington had urged him to do it. A woman in Washington, who wanted him, but wanted him emotionally clean. Whatever that meant.

Leon knew the facts. Not the state department's rendition of the facts, which spurred decisions that, by some accounts, cost a million Tutsis their lives. It was a fact that two months into the genocide the West refused to act.

U.S. State Department officials played word games confirming individual cases or "acts of" genocide but not full-scale attacks by the Hutu party. Leon was aware of the fact that the U.S. was legally obliged by its signatory status during the 1948 Convention on Genocide Repression. If genocide was taking place, the U.S. was obliged by international law to stop it. Unfortunately, the small U.N. force deployed in Rwanda as part of an original peace settlement, was told not to intervene. The West retreated with fresh memories of Somalia. American casualties had soured public opinion. Supporting the Tutsis would have cost money and blood. It wasn't going to happen.

Leon was one of the first Western reporters to arrive in Rwanda two months into the frenzied mass murder.

June 1994
Rwanda

Maria was wearing a tan smock. She looked her fifteen years. She had considerable time in the hospital after losing her hand thwarting a head blow. Before that, she had lived under rubble coming out only at night to get food. Her captors, once they'd cut her, presumed her for dead. They met in the church where her parents were killed.

"I'm Leon," he'd said. Her gaze shifted from him to the woven mats scattered on the floor. Her sadness bore down on him like weight. She was alone. She was afraid. What could he do for her?

He remembered that week spent by her side, that week in June of 1994. He remembered their lovemaking. "Who would want me now?" she had asked. The bandages had been removed from her face and hands. Her healing wounds were exposed. Her skin seemed almost transparent, sheer, like the wings of an insect.

"Will you give me a child?" she had asked.

He remembered reaching out and cushioning her with his arms. She felt frail, like a picnic chair that could collapse any moment. The rain fell. The smell of death floated in the air. He was surprised her request did not surprise him.

"How will you take care of this child?" he asked.

"My Savior will," she said.

Your Savior couldn't take care of the thousand Tutsis killed in this church, Leon thought, suddenly realizing he was projecting his own inability onto God.

Leon was a lonely man. His heart pressed dry. The life steamed out of it. He needed to bleed, to feel alive again.

He thought, *Over this odd world, this is the half of the world that's dark now. I have to hunt a thing that lives on tears.*

She had trembled when they'd made love. He was, at that moment, all she had, and so this act of love was as important to him as it was to her. For the first time in ages he felt articulated. He wasn't writing. Writing was a way of having experiences without the scars. Instead he was living. She had asked him this favor. This one favor that might sustain her. And so he had made love to her, this fifteen-year-old virgin, who, by some ineffable instinct, knew she would bear his child.

February 1997
Rwanda

He said thank you to the cafe's owner in Kirwandese. He opened the torn screen door of the hut, held it for Maria to pass through first. Beer bottles littered the outside. A fog lingered over the red hills. They began to walk.

"So which is most important," he asked her, "justice or mercy?"

"Justice will not bring back the dead."

The survivors. He thought of an Escher painting. Characters marginalized, within margins, within margins.

As they walked, a group of adolescent girls with shaved heads emerged from a shack surrounded with barbed wire. They spun around Leon, circling him.

"Money!" one cried. Another sang, "There are no virgins left in Nyarubuye." They laughed and then scattered like sugar.

"My home is not far from here," Maria said sadly.

Love is not a feeling. It is a decision. Why had this thought come into his head? Hadn't Sylvia asked him a variation of this same question, what love felt like? The earth under his feet was soft, pliable. He made footprints in the mud. Maria didn't. How odd, he thought, how very odd.

"I pray to forgive, but I want to remember," Maria said. "I don't want to become numb like Hutus who felt nothing as they murdered. I don't want this experience to become a cloud-blur."

"A cloud-blur," he repeated.

Leon remembered a funeral of a former classmate. An Irish tenor had sung "Danny Boy". An angel chorus was piped in. He remembered feeling sickened. As if what the funeral guests were feeling wasn't enough.

Maria stopped and faced him. "This is my find," Maria said, "To the extent that I know pain, I can know joy."

A truck piled high with bags of charcoal passed them. Two Ankole cows languished on the grass. He stumbled on the shell of a spent grenade.

"I am sorry," he said. Her gaze drifted to a circle of sticks, the remains of a fire, beneath her. "I am so sorry," he repeated.

The sun hemorrhaged in the African sky.

"I knew you had only one week in Rwanda. I knew you had to go back to the States."

"I knew you were pregnant," he said.

"Men know so many things," she said.

Hers was an agile passion, he remembered.

"Is there a woman in America?" she asked.

"Are we near your home?" he answered.

Children on the road scrawled in the dirt. He noticed their callused feet.

He thought of his feeling for Maria. Was it guilt he was feeling? He stopped walking and turned to face her.

It was she who spoke first. "I love my daughter for the same reason you love me," she said.

On the other side of the road, a woman with a foam mattress balanced on her head walked barefoot. How many miles had she pressed on, uphill?

It wasn't a time thing, Leon thought. *You could be with someone three hours, three minutes, and love him or her.* And who was to say he and Maria weren't meant to be together? Yes, she was this, and he was that, yet she inspired wisdom in him at odds with her youth. She was profoundly simple. But he had left her. He had not communicated with her since returning to the States to resume reporting. Yes, it had disturbed him. His actions had disturbed him. If it hadn't been for Sylvia he might not be here now.

They sat down on the gravel. Shrouded by the faded light of winter, Leon said, "I can't stay forever, Maria."

June 1994

On his first visit to Rwanda Leon came into contact with the many of the killers. They were manning roadblocks, loitering around municipal buildings, stationed at army encampments. Many looked crazed.

He got around in an old jeep. He had started in Kabale, Uganda, approximately fifty miles north of Kigale, Rwanda's capital. He swerved past clusters of goats, small herds of emaciated cattle, banana groves, and children peddling cokes or the occasional skewer of days-old meat. He visualized the ransacked villages he would pass deeper into Rwanda. He had a map. He knew about the roving bands. He knew military gangs nested in the swamps and forests, military gangs who would leave gin bottles and dirty clothes behind. Having a passport was a joke. He knew he could be killed any moment.

He carried a beat-up short-wave radio and could usually get the BBC World Service news although the signal was spotty. From this battered radio, he learned when Hutu militia seized Kigali, Rwanda's capital. As the Tutsi RPF rebels advanced they discovered thousands of bodies in churches and community halls. A bizarre thought occurred to him. *Who would harvest the avocados?*

Rwanda's main road was smooth. The European Union spent money resurfacing the highway, at a time when President Habyarimana was receiving huge sums of foreign aid. They built a sturdy tar road to Kigali, which then branched off to Burundi, Tanzania, and Zaire. *A few months ago before he'd arrived the road had been one of the great veins of Central Africa. Now it was empty.* Weird, Leon thought, *a kind of tropical Chernobyl.* Leon's priority at that time in Rwanda was getting clearance at the RPF's headquarters, a defunct tea plantation, in Mulindi.

February 1997

Vines climbed the outside walls of Maria's mud-brick bungalow. In the distance loomed the clay-streaked hills; squares of vegetation, the sweet-potato fields, the compound where the corn-man lived, and the well where people drew their water.

Maria's living room was sparse. Resting on a plywood table near the entrance, were two cloth frames containing photos of her parents. A wicker chair stood alone. A playpen with a clean white blanket slung over the side rested in the center of the room. Some LPs were stacked on a blond wooden shelf. He noticed the album jacket of *Miles Davis Live*.

"My aunt usually takes care of Noel when I teach, but Auntie is with our cousin in Kibungo. Would you mind to stay here for a little while? Please rest, make yourself at ease, and I will fetch Noel from my neighbor who lives in the village."

Neighbors, Leon thought. *Wasn't kindness the basis for civilization?*

A realistic painting of a silver fish, a combination of oil, gouache, and watercolor hung in the living room, adjoining the small bedroom. The painting jarred his memory of Sylvia and her fish story. He recalled cars he'd seen in the States, their rear bumpers sporting a metallic fish, the symbol for Jesus Christ.

Was this what scientists referred to as morphological resonance? Harmonic convergence? A coincidence of events intended to mean something. Synchronicity? He felt embarrassed. The comparison seemed so strained. He bemoaned the apartheid between science, which tried to explain coincidence, and religion, which felt it never needed to.

"Tell me about the fish," he said.

Twice in the past few months he'd heard of two million-dollar art collections being sold because the owners were finally secure enough to realize they never liked or understood what was on their walls.

"I've grown more concerned for the butchers than the butchered. The butchered are in a state of grace," Maria said.

Stalin's famous remark, like a juggernaut, flashed in his head. "One death was a tragedy. A million deaths a mere statistic."

Rwanda's tribal full-scale genocide attempt barely made the six-o'clock news. What of this culture of hate? He was curious. Was it temporary insanity, what Aldous Huxley called "herd intoxication"?

Certainly, Habyarimana's henchmen, through newspapers, radio, and vitriolic oratory had stirred the pot, vowing that all Tutsis were members of a fifth column, that given the opportunity, would steal their land and subordinate the Hutus to field service once more.

When had this culture of impunity developed? There'd been killings predating killings. For centuries the peasants had been taught to follow orders. Obedience became oxygen to them. The killing of the Tutsis became the civic duty of the Hutus. To the impoverished masses the message became: "Kill Tutsis, and your problems will be over." But who could kill like this? Even with ample provocation and prejudice? After all, the Hutus weren't born any more immoral than the rest of us. Was being groomed to kill— living in a society that implicitly licensed murder, then later, staging the entrance of a few motivational speakers, all that was required?

The child looked like him. She was dressed in a purple cotton jumper.

"*C'est ton pere*," Maria said to Noel. "I speak French to her—and English."

He remembered the night Noel was conceived. Black forms flickered on the edge of twilight. Bats dove into the silver Eucalyptus.

Noel waved a hair comb in front of his face.

"She wants you to comb her hair," Maria said.

Leon gently took the comb. Starting at the crown of her small head he moved the tortoise shell implement through her black hair.

Over and over he combed her hair. As if repeating a mantra, the action assumed a hypnotic quality for him. He felt perfectly suited to this intimate service.

By now Noel had fallen asleep in his arms. Maria came over and kissed him first on the forehead and then on the lips. Her tongue was a wafer in his mouth

The situation was this: In December of 1996, shortly after the mass return from border camps, Rwanda had finally begun holding genocide trials. The judicial system was overstretched. Ninety thousand Hutus, accused of genocide, awaiting trial, were crammed in jails. Only four defense lawyers were available. Of those accused, only one man, who was single handedly responsible for catalyzing the mass slaughter was finally brought to trail. Karamara, a wealthy Hutu who financed the militia's killing sprees in hundreds of places like Nyarubuye, was sentenced to death on February 14, 1997.

He had no guilt regarding "blood on his hands" when asked about the genocide. Later he amended his statement saying, "There was no genocide." In jail, Karamara said flatly, "As soon as we get the chance we will continue where we left off."

February 1997

Leon woke with Maria in his arms. He looked out the window at the rain, the pale sky, the metal-colored mist, a sheath over the tea plantations miles away. He watched Maria as she got dressed into a cap-sleeved, rose-colored blouse and a *pagne*, tight and smooth around her pelvis. She wore white tennis shoes. He studied her as she retrieved a small, heavy iron to press his khaki shorts.

"Tutsi neighbors and some sympathetic Hutus have been kind to us. They give us chickens, tomatoes." Her feet were long and thin. Hutus had cut off the feet of the Tutsis because the Tutsis were taller. "Tall trees," they'd cried, excitedly, "cut them down!" One machete swoop was sometimes all it took. If the blade was sharp.

He had written a poem about trees when he was younger. In the poem the trees spoke to their violators.

> With penknives you carved hearts,
> Raw valentines
> You made love on our soil
> When the rain fell like stones
> We stood tall, marked with your names
> But now we are scant and thinned
> Our veins collapsing like gun-shot birds
> What happened to our elegant lives?
> Our trunks are bleeding fire for you
> Swollen suns sink into violent houses
> The birds are bones-on-fire wailing
> We are afraid
> What can we do?
> What can we do to ease your pain?

Often, he thought, actors of violence were the ones hurting, the ones in pain. But in Rwanda, the killers seemed to enjoy the killing, unless they were tired from the grueling physical exertion. Then they merely appeared exhausted.

Noel had woken up. She wobbled toward her Raggedy Ann doll resting in a decorative basket made from palm fronds. She picked up the doll and held it high over her head. She ran to Leon.

"Breakfast?" asked Maria.

"I'm famished," he said. He was not fond of gruel.

"Famished?" she laughed, "What is 'famished?'" With a long match she lit a fire under a pot of boiling water.

"*Pour toi*," Noel said.

He accepted Noel's gift of the doll. The doll's hand had been cut off and the cloth arm filled with wheat hulls, carefully stitched at the wrist.

"She wanted a *Mommy* doll, with one hand missing, so I made her one," Maria said.

He needed to go to Kigali, one hundred kilometers, around fifty miles northwest of Nyarubuye. Funds were being wired to him by way of the *Banque Commerciale du Rwanda*. He had been advised traveling was dangerous.

He heard a sound outside the wooden door of the bungalow and peered out a cracked window. A bony man in a stained shirt roasted corn in a pan of hot coals. He looked at Leon and from the gutter of his throat he growled, "*Olienyamasw!*"

"We are all in danger," Maria said. "Froduald Karamira was just sentenced, and bands of *Interhamwe* (those who band together), many of whom were in Zaire, are killing again. Even Hutus who were kind to Tutsis in 1994 are being massacred. Just last month, in the northwestern province of Ruhengeri, three Spanish aid workers and a Canadian priest were shot to death, the first killings of Westerners since the genocide."

"So what does it mean?" he asked, "What that man said?"

"It means 'You were sired by animals.'"

That evening he wrote in his journal, a leather book Sylvia had given him: *What is Maria thinking? At what moment does one fall in love? Or is it a series of moments? And how is that different from being in love?*

What was it he felt for her? Genuine care? Physical attraction? Awe? Curiosity? Pity? The French author Balzac, he remembered, said the hardest sentiment to endure was pity, especially when it was deserved.

Was love an art? Requiring knowledge and effort? Or was it a feeling? Something one finds if one is fortunate? *People think that loving is simple,* he thought, *but finding the right object to love, or be loved by, is difficult.* He'd memorized Paraclesus.

He who knows nothing loves nothing. He who can do nothing understands nothing. He who understands nothing is worthless. But he who understands also loves, notices, sees. The more knowledge is inherent in a thing, the greater the love. Anyone who imagines that all fruits ripen at the same time as the strawberry knows nothing about love.

The fruit metaphor was obvious, but when he reconsidered it, could mean just about anything. *I know nothing about love*, Leon wrote.

What did Maria know?

She had slid right past that state of euphoria that characterized new and uncharted territory. He thought of Froduald Kamirama. Everything he'd said was a lie, including the words 'and' and 'the'. He thought of the phantasmagoric, Hieronymous Bosche-like hell that described Rwanda. He'd written one theory of love in his diary. He had no idea whose theory it was:

> If we want to learn how to love we must proceed in the same way we have to if we want to learn any other art, say music, or the art of medicine. To become a master in any art, that art must be of ultimate concern.

Some people, Leon figured, had a gene for loving. People incapable of love lived long lives, pickled by their own vinegar. As for himself, the more mature he became, the more he understood his limitless gift for what Freud called *normal misery*.

After the massacre in 1994, extremist Hutu leaders followed the Tutsis into exile. In refugee camps set up by the International community Hutus who organized the genocide became camp leaders. One million headed to camps In Zaire, Burundi, and Tanzania. US troops provided water, food, and medicine, insuring the comfort of killers from places like Nyarubuye. A deep unease in the international community swelled. One million dollars a day were spent reinforcing the policy of the killers. In two and a half years, the total reached one billion dollars. Money earmarked for food and aid was spent to buy arms and train military to relaunch a Hutu attack on Rwanda. The camps were finally closed at the end of 1996.

February 1997

Maria made goat stew for dinner. She carefully shredded pieces for Noel and fed her small spoonfuls.

"Watch for the tiny bones," she told Leon.

Noel and Maria taught Leon a song in French, Rwanda's *lingua franca*. It was about Napoleon. "Why would you sing about Napoleon?" Leon had asked. "He was a creepster!"

"You teach us a song then!" So he taught them, "Bugaloo Down Broadway", a seventies R&B tune. Maria snapped her fingers. Noel swayed back and forth. The rain fell on the tin roof, percussive, metered. He stared at Maria.

"You weep for joy?" she asked him.

Maria bathed Noel in a large aluminum tub. A yellow plastic duck floated wantonly on the water.

"You're right, Maria; Rwanda's a mess. The RPF troops can't control the situation. The Hutus fight the RPF then retreat into their villages in the northwest. They're handing out flyers with the usual messages, "Kill all Tutsis," "Send them to Abyssinia!""

He recalled staring into the Akagera River on his first visit to Nyarubuye, brown from upland silt, dense with elephant grass, before he saw the bodies, bobbing up and down like blow-up dolls. The river runs from the highlands of Rwanda through the stomach of the country until it crosses the border into Tanzania and then Uganda, funneling finally into Lake Victoria. The river brimmed with the dead. From days in the water the bloated bodies looked white. Ugandan fisherman collected the corpses, thousands in number, to provide proper burials.

"It's in some sense, the greed of the Hutus," Maria said to him, "not wanting to give up their old ideas. When a foreigner asks me what happened, I say poor people killed the ones who weren't so poor. Hutus see history through the prism of their pigment, which is darker than ours. Can we help that we are lighter or taller? And look as if our ancestors came from Egypt? Maybe this war is biblical. Maybe we are victims of ancestral memory. We are still Rwandans."

First stop on his first visit to Nyarubuye, situated near the Tanzanian border, was Rusomo Commune where the RPF (Tutsi "rebels") had set up a reception center for Tutsi refugees. At that point, he ditched his jeep and wended his way through the bush. Near the whitewashed church, he eyed a scrim of thick savannah grass threaded with thorn bush and acadia. The odor of decay made him gag. A white marble statue of Christ hovered over the door. Clouds of gnats made it hard for him to see.

"The first time I saw you, I didn't think you would live. They couldn't stop the gangrene." Leon clasped his arms around Maria's waist. He pulled her tightly to him. Noel splashed and cooed. Leon kissed Maria's neck. She smelled of cardamom and linseed. Around her neck she wore a strand of Persian turquoise he'd brought from the States and had hidden in his pocket while traveling through Rwanda. If Hutus had seen it, they would have seized it.

"Very good turquoise," he had told Maria, "no visible veins."

That night seated on a cot, he stared at the bolt of mosquito netting he had purchased the day before, enough to protect three people while they slept. *The netting is supple,* he thought and then suddenly became aware of her presence. She was now sitting beside him. A kerosene lantern, resting on a bruised fruitwood table, burned. Maria's face assumed the secret glow of an apple in a Flemish painting. How it happened he did not know but all at once something seized him and flung him at her feet. He wanted to speak but could not. What had happened to his larynx?

I came to see the damage that was done and the treasures that prevail, he thought, *piece by piece I seem to re-enter the world.*

He woke at dawn and watched them sleep. He felt connected to Maria and Noel, the way the heart is connected to the lungs; the way the skin is an umbrella organ for systems of great magnitude. By the faint morning light he wrote in his dairy:

> *What does God want? I struggle with my faith. Why did God allow Rwanda's tragedy? Some say God had nothing to do with this. They are letting God off the hook, I guess, in His defense. An honorable stance, that is, to be a character witness. But one that defies the sovereignty of God. The notion that certain evils happen without God's permission implies that He is powerless to stop them. The logical extension to this line of reasoning is that God is weak and subject to the ravages of sin.*
>
> *Maria has faith. If faith is a gift why is it given to some and not to others? That doesn't seem very democratic of God. Maria quotes scripture, I have set my face like flint knowing I will not be put to shame. I am shamed that my faith is not a larger vessel. The larger the vessel, the more grace it can accommodate. Why do some receive more grace than others? Didn't God decide His preferred customers before we were born? Of course, we applaud our free will. But how free is it, if some are gifted with a good nature? I am naturally choleric and shifty, prone to rule and to control. Now take someone like Maria. Isn't it easier for her to enter heaven because of her natural disposition? Isn't she less likely to sin because she was born with a beneficent temperament? Or does God grade on effort? And why are we so presumptuous to attempt to understand these issues when God's cosmological expertise by definition dwarfs ours? It's like trying to explain calculus to a toddler. How bold of us to try to get it! After all, He is God. My Catholic faith taught me to honor the*

"Mystery." Anything the Catholics can't explain, they call a mystery. Which is very smart of them.

I once asked a bartender if he thought God was a Democrat or a Republican. He said, "God is both because He is everything."

"No," I said, "He is not everything because he is not evil."

"Well, then he's a Democrat," the bartender replied.

If God gives me grace or blessings because I do good and am good, my free will is not entirely free (i.e. neutral and unbiased) because it is influenced by His grace. To complicate matters even more, if God is all loving why aren't people who aren't good, either by natural inclination or by choice, privy to his grace the same his followers are? Yet God cavorted with sinners. He said he preferred a real sinner to a tepid Christian. I can understand his preference. Sinners are usually more fun.

When is righteous anger allowed? Is anger ever righteous? Why can't we answer these questions? Because God doesn't deal the obvious hand. It would require too little of us. Am I right?

We keep asking God to tell us His will. Should we turn left or right? Take this job or that job. Stay single or marry? I wonder if the risen Christ doesn't shrug His shoulders and say, "You know we have the big stuff taken care of now. You are forgiven and freed. So make a choice and surprise me."

I know that whichever job I take, whichever woman I marry, He will bless me. But I want to be in right alignment with the Master plan.

The morning light swims through the small window in this room. I am somehow emerging a different man, on this African soil, in this African light. I ask Him in very precise language, "What is it You want from me?"

June 1994

Radios blasted in Kigali. "Tutsis are in the Air Burundi Office on Rue De Lac Nasho. Tutsis are in the Bank on Avenue de Rusumo. Go and kill them."

In Nyrabuye, Maria, bludgeoned and left for dead, lay motionless among the bodies. She came out at night to find food and water and in the morning returned to chase away the rats, dogs, pigs, from the corpses. The Hutus championed their progress. *Tugire gukora akazi*: "Let's go do the work." Some Tutsis paid to be shot rather than be hacked by machetes or *masus*, clubs spiked with nails.

Leon, in Central Africa for the first time, was afraid of catching malaria, so he swallowed Larium pills. The pills were hallucinogenic, producing a kind of synesthesia for him. A big, green-colored semi reminded him of purgatory. Two women, dressed in pungent colors, carried large clay pots on their heads diverted his attention. He was able to smell the colors of their garments. Red smelled like pomade. Blue smelled like the word "please." At the market, he could buy a half dozen hamsters. Africans bred hamsters to eat. Tasted like chicken, they said. *So did goat, frog, rabbit, rattlesnake and many mammals, come to think of it*, he thought. He bought a citronella candle from a woman with swollen limbs. He thought of party balloons filled with water. Her legs and arms were shapes he could hear. Music! Not a requiem or a dirge, but a sonata. Beethoven's "Moonlight Sonata", to be specific.

February 1997

"I have to teach class today," Maria said, "We have a hair-braiding clinic today."

"A what?"

"We pretend the clinic is in Los Angeles, so we practice our English."

Maria paused for air, inhaled and exhaled. "I teach in a small room in the church. Skulls, spines, leg-bones have not been moved from the floor. Leathery bodies slump together. The Hutu *bourgmestre* insists on keeping them there, as memorials to the dead, but he is secretly proud of these terrible skeletons. The *bourgmestre*, as you know, was in charge of the Hutu village before the massacre. Unfortunately, he still has some input. The RPF *conseiller* stationed at our sector office says this is—"

A dark pall, the shadow of a crow, flew over Leon's face.

"Some of the young are very bruised emotionally. They see Jesus on the cross. And I say to them, 'He died for you.' I tell them there is plenty in heaven. Melons, mangos, pineapples, the sweetest almonds, the juiciest raisins. They love heaven! Then one asks me, 'What are all the bodies still doing on the floor?'

"Another asks me, whom did my mommy die for, whom did my daddy die for? Did they die for me too?' Then I pray to the Holy Spirit to give me the words I need. *Because I have none.*

"Would you like to watch Noel? For a few hours while I teach? You and she can go to the marketplace." He remembered the market smells, his first time in this small country, right in the heart of Africa, practically sitting on the equator. The smell of mildew, of charcoal-burned meat, of old sweat, tobacco, and fruit rind. He remembered the terra cotta hills looming large from where he'd stood, the rooftops of palm and thatch. He remembered the piercing Rasta music.

Now he had a daughter. He felt propelled like a chord sprung from a steel guitar. He had never felt this way with his son. Perhaps everything was timing. Leon was changing. In his diary that evening he wrote:

> *God is not found along a continuum but in isolated moments. The hammer of a heartbeat, for example. Let me be no stranger to these ordinary habits of loving.*

Maria stacked the dry dishes on the kitchen shelf. "There is only one phone in the village in the sector office occupied by the RPF," she said. He knew this already but said nothing. "Electricity comes on and off. I will cook *de la viande en brochette* for us tonight."

What, he wanted to know, *had kept her alive?* Those days underneath the bodies.

He remembered the market of concrete stalls, pitch-black men drinking *urwagna* with reed straws stuck in a trough. He remembered the battered brick building's awning that read *Saloon de Coiffure*. He remembered 12 year olds selling AK-47s.

"You can ask me simple things," she'd replied, "such as, 'Why are there so many cows and no milk on our table?' or, 'What does fifteen hundred francs buy in Nyrabuye?' or, "Why don't you paint your lips?' But you ask me what kept me alive! I will tell you. Many things. I thought of my mother, how she loved to hear me talk. My hair had begun to fall out; I was going—I don't know the English word—'bald'? I wanted to grow my hair again. *I was waiting for you to see my hair.* That kept me alive. I thought of other girls who had lost both feet. I had lost only a hand. When the Hutus had gone home, their work done for the day, I rested, under a scarf of stars. Can I say that? A scarf of stars? I asked God what was going to happen to me.

'Be still and know that I am God,' he answered. I embraced my suffering. It was my task, and I had to handle it in my unique way. I spoke to the children. I mothered them. Their eyes stung from crying. I collected their tears in an imaginary cup.

"Does all this sound so poetic? So intriguing? I am just a girl, still just a girl. You think I am a woman but," she began to cry. She cried in his arms until darkness surrounded them. A concentrated stillness opened up like a strange exotic flower in the center of the room. In the center of the room and *in him*. What did he hear? Columns of air moving when she breathed? The batting of her eyelashes against his face?

"I would find brambles to put on these shallow graves to scare away the wild pigs."

"Where were the dogs?"

She paused and looked away. "They killed the dogs because they were eating the dead."

"Two sugars with your tea?" she asked him.

"Yes, please," he answered.

"Our baby-to-come kept me alive," she said.

If he had done anything in his life that made him feel worthy to breathe in the thick air of consequence, it was this. The earth could stop spinning, and he would know that he had had one overwhelming purpose. Her. He had made the decision to love her.

"And lemon, I remember," she said. She squeezed the small lemon into the ceramic cup.

"I will say this with certainty. God chooses his favorites to suffer. 'Blessed are the sorrowful for theirs is the kingdom of heaven. Blessed are those who mourn.' He has special affection for those who endure so much. Wouldn't the father of a crippled child show that child extra love and mercy? God does the same. Those in pain are his prized ones."

"This life is short. Seventy years? The next one never ends. I would rather endure my trials now."

"You're saying *happy* people are *wait listed* for heaven?" Leon asked.

"How do I tell you? The suffering is *sweet*. I can't explain this to you. Like Dizzie Gillespie said when someone asked him to define 'jazz'—'Some things you just have to experience.'"

He thought of women he had fallen in love with. The heady lightness he found losing himself in them was an escape. Falling in love was like being an addict. The whole brain map changed. Pleasure centers were sparked with neural electrical energy. For three years anyway. He'd read that in some women's magazine. But this escape, like any drug, never worked. Because in the end you always were left with yourself, and, if you were lucky enough to believe, God. If people accused you of using Him as a drug, you'd say, "Amen. So be it." You still were stuck with yourself, and life wasn't any less painful.

It was a shopworn phrase, but, "Another person cannot make you happy," was an axiom he finally understood. And once one understood that, one was free to allow himself to be happy, *whatever his situation*. If someone special then stumbled into your force field, you were simply ready for the next set of challenges.

He took a bite of marzipan pastry she'd pulled from a tin.

"Anise?" he asked. She guided each bite into his mouth.

"If a thief stole my baby would I die? Tiny little deaths strung like beads, yes, but eventually, I would find peace. I have been through the sewer and found a diamond. How many people can say this?"

"So, you are happy?"

"I am more interested in a life of meaning than a 'happy' life. What is 'happy'? Joy is better. If life has meaning then it is joyful in the pain."

"And you'll love me if I leave again?"

"Love is not erased so easily as a pencil drawing. When you leave me I will love you."

She stared at the sturdy contours of his face. "I try not to think about tomorrow. God will give me *that* strength when I need it, not before."

She wound a strand of her hair around her finger. "God works in contradictions," she explained, "but in His economy everything evolves toward the good."

After a long pause he asked, "Even exterminations?"

"Cholera was a problem in Goma."

"Why are you changing the subject?"

"90,000 Hutus who fled to relief camps twenty miles from Rwanda's border were killers who were given food, blankets, and money by relief people who did not know the angels from the devils." Her head fell as if her memory were suddenly too heavy for her neck.

"What is it?" he asked.

"My mother and father; I see their faces when I sleep. The blood on the bamboo spears that blinded them. Their feet cut off by Hutus who did not want them to be so tall. Do you know what I did? I buried my mother's feet under the shade of an old pine. I buried my father's feet—O Why? Why, this extravagance of sorrows?"

She pressed her head to his chest and began to cry; then her breathing became jerky, almost seismic. He would remember the feeling of moisture on his skin, through his shirt, from her tears. For fifty minutes she cried, fifty minutes, the time it takes for bread to leaven, and then her limp body collapsed in his arms. While she slept he prayed.

When she opened her eyes, she said, "I have no velvet chaise for you. I have a rattan cot."

A rattan cot, he thought.

Leon's mouth felt dry. The sweet starch had made him thirsty. Maria had boiled some water and bottled it for him. He walked over to the corked carafe on the plywood table then returned to her.

"Hutus could steal everything from me but my thoughts. My thoughts were mine!" She wrapped her arms around his neck. She hugged him with all her strength. Tears dove down her cheeks.

He had heard that people speak in iambic pentameter when they have important things to say. "I am right and you are wrong." She could have said *that* to her assailants.

Now she was sitting beside him. Their hips and shoulders were touching. He took another sip of water and swallowed.

"You see," she began, and turned her body to face him. "Everyone must know what happened. Your story must be real, as only you can tell it, not just what you have seen with your eyes and heard with your ears but what you have felt. Your voice must be a clarion. Because the truth is far beyond journalism's grasp."

He never saw her again. On her way to school, one man, a Hutu vagrant, killed her. She was shot with a Russian Tokarev. She was buried in a clean muslin cloth.

For days he faltered. He felt haunted, ugly, and exaggerated. He bruised himself bumping into furniture. One moment bled into the next. He had trouble remembering things. Had he showered? Had he shaved? *Was that her white undershirt he carried in his hands from room to room?* Was that her voice, her words? "I have failed at dying. I am with you."

He had to exit the country. He feared his own assassination. He would take the child and flee back to the States. This would be the beginning of another story. He could return to journalism because he had *lived* the story. He *was* the story, complete with an antagonist, protagonist, and a child.

The work of becoming a human being. He had blithely escaped it once. Liberia had done such a number on him he had just checked out, neutralized, let everything wash over him like water. Now his latent sense of loss arrived like a stone in his stomach. He was familiar with the theory that we arrive at truth by way of our own disillusionments. If suffering defined what it meant to be a human being, he had learned, after Liberia, to become a thing.

What he was feeling couldn't be only Maria's death. It was a host of deaths. The death of the world he had known, his youth, his idealist impulses, his marriage, the hope his son would ever be socialized, the death of the notions that righteousness begot righteousness and that the world made sense. He had never mourned these losses in their time. Add to that the death of Liberian children and a million Tutsis. He'd just moved on as quickly as possible, donning the appropriate armor needed for the next gig. To become impervious was the goal he'd met with desultory goodwill. Now he was experiencing the death of even that victory. These were multiple deaths he was now grieving. Why else would his grief be this intense?

Why? Because he didn't want to love her so much? Now that she was gone? What exactly was happening to him? This fusillade of emotions, where was it coming from? Where would it go?

"You ask me about exterminations," she'd said. "I don't know. I don't know. Why does the moon have a pock-marked face? Who am *I* to question God?"

He thought, "Man is borne into trouble as the sparks fly upward.*"*

PART THREE
SYLVIA'S DIARY

February 1997
Sylvia's Diary
Washington D.C.

"Being dead is normal," a Rwandan refugee says into the television camera. I watch a documentary. The dead are scattered in the fields. They become the atmosphere.

Leon left yesterday for Rwanda. I wanted him to stay but encouraged him to go. Of course he and I are always dueling, and I imagine, at least for me, this intellectual ping-pong is a shield. Don't get too close to the tetrahedron that lies beneath my casing. My girlfriend says that relying on a man to manage a relationship is like handing a scalpel to a monkey and saying, "Operate."

"So, how does a woman manage a relationship?" I ask her.

"Try being vulnerable," Elizabeth answers. What she says makes sense, but I don't like it. Why do I have to be the guinea pig? Elizabeth teaches *Ashtanga* Yoga. She has specific ideas about men and women. I told her when I turned thirteen, unhappy with my new voluptuousness; I bound my bosom with adhesive tape. She said I was protecting my heart.

I would like to be authentic with Leon. The night before he left for Rwanda he complimented me on my "sexy camisole". I replied it was comfortable and the color, puce, a dark red, was a favorite. "Why can't you just say you're just wearing it for me?" he asked. I *was* wearing it for him.

I can hear him now, the brillo-pad tone in his voice. "Why are you always messing with me? You get right up there in that bully pulpit and do that ex-cathedra thing."

Why do I need to compete with him?

"Outwitting me doesn't make me like you any better," he said.
I *could* say, "I love you."

Was I vulnerable with my first love, Lars? Lars had been recruited to play hockey for Dartmouth. (I'm with those ancient Greeks who placed physical culture on a top shelf with myth and drama.) I'd applied to Dartmouth because, at the time, the male female ratio was three to one, and Dartmouth men were known throughout the Ivy League for being good-looking athletes: outdoorsy and smart.

Lars, and his dog Jack were an indissoluble team on campus. I finally met the two of them at a *Heoret* Halloween party where one of Lars' frat brothers tried to blow up a hot water bottle. (The spider veins in his collapsed cheeks turned puce.) Walking up the stairs of the house, I heard boots behind me. "I'm following you," a voice said, as Lars squarely grabbed my hips. Jack the Dog pulled me aside moments later and said, "My master is such a dog. Don't give it up for him. You may be a good woman but all he sees is a pair of tight Levis that wandered into his force field."

"I need a boyfriend," I told Lars weeks after our hooking up.
"You don't need a boyfriend. You need a sex partner."
"I don't want a sex partner."
"You're too needy. Your neediness makes you aggressive. Men like vulnerable women."
"I'm vulnerable."
"I don't want to hurt you."
"Then why are we seeing one another?"
"Maybe we should stop."
"You're willing to stop?"
"If that's what you need."

We continued our affair. Those mornings when I woke up before he did, I'd want to touch his shoulder, wrap my arm around his waist, but was afraid he might push me away. Other times he'd favor my affection. Everything depended on his mood, which I had trouble reading. *Maybe,* I thought, *I should buy him a mood ring.*

"Examine your sense of entitlement," my German female psychiatrist said.
"Do you think I feel entitled?"
"It's not what I think that matters," she said.
Wait a minute, I thought. *Aren't I paying her for her professional opinion?*
Actually my sense of entitlement is exaggerated. I feel deserving. Leon thinks the opposite, thinks that I settle for less because at the root of myself, that's all I feel I deserve.

"Why else, Sylvia, would you date young men who move their lips when they read?"

Had drinks today with an acquaintance (who graduated from Princeton the same year I graduated from Dartmouth) at Café Deluxe, a restaurant bar on Wisconsin Avenue, His uncle is a priest, he's Catholic, and so were his former football buddies who joined us. We started talking about Catholicism, and I said I didn't consider myself an apostate. One of them asked me, "When you marry then, you will obey your husband?"
"What do you think Jesus means in the gospels when he speaks of a man and a woman being equally yoked?" I answered.

Doctors are dispensing antidepressants like Pez. One third of congress takes a daily SSRI. Trent, a woman I run into at Starbucks, takes the highest recommended dose. The first time she came over to say hello, I noticed her eyebrows moved up and down like Venetian blinds. Very Chaplinesque, I thought. She sported big silicone breasts that she admitted had a problem leaking. Initially I thought they looked grotesque, but her sweetness, almost impossible to exaggerate, suppressed my urge to judge her further.

"Dale" (the cargo pilot she sees, mostly late at night), "picked me out of a crowd at Café Milano because of these breasts!" she said over her tall chai.

"You'd look better without them," I said.

A wave of anger shimmied over her face. Her eyes watered. She covered her face with her hands. I rose from my seat, my eyes watering too, and whispered, "I'm sorry." And I truly was, and am, so sorry for all of us. Women desperate for male attention are the most fragile.

She fears Dale is with her mostly for the sex, but that's what she's advertising. "I don't want a serious relationship," she says. The truth is she would give her cuspids for Dale to care.

What is disappointing is this: Women are wired for meaningful relationships, because we have the heart for them. In this postfeminine age we think we have to be like men in an effort to compete with them, when what we should be doing is leading by example. A quality relationship includes the whole person. Why should we settle for just a *zipless f*—(my apologies to Erica Jong) trying to beat men at their own game? We won't win. They are too good at it. Why would we want to "use" men the way some men "use" us? Does that improve our relationships? Does that improve society?

What is going on with Trent is that she doesn't feel worthy of a decent relationship. So she lies and says things like, "Why would I want to marry a cargo pilot? They are the truck drivers of the airways." Trent wants Dale to love her for more than her pneumatic breasts. I think the tears were about her recognizing this truth. She got angry because she realized she was deceiving herself. "To thine own self be true," is a crucial axiom.

Joe, a friend who happens to be a retina surgeon, came over for a batch of frozen margaritas (a splash of *cointreau* is key) I had blended in my new Waring. He grew up tatter-poor (food and clothes were a luxury), with two brothers and a sister, in the mountains of Appalachia. He had a story to tell. Told me one day his mother had woken the kids for school and realized Joe, seven at the time, had no clean clothes. Rather than have Joe wear his dirty clothes to school, his mother made him wear a clean dress belonging to his sister.

I imagined the scene. Boys roughhousing in the school lot. Joe crouched outside the barbed wire fence, eyes red-rimmed. Joe, crouched in the weeds, crouched in the weeds, shamed.

Sky-frail boy, head hung low like a platinum moon, like a platinum moon in a crimson sky.

"Who's Afraid of Red" is a jazz riff I hear when I reach that second horizon of feeling.

"Hold tight," I said, "I'll be back in an hour." I poured the last of my *Heradura* tincture into a to-go cup and cabbed it to the Armani Exchange in Georgetown. I summoned the male clerk, and with enthusiasm (enthusiasm, by the way, means "filled with God") said, "Show me the most manly suit you have in 38 long." His choice: a manifestly perfect black duo. "Wrap it up; I'll take it," I sang, Joe Tex style. "Oh, and add this, please," I said, handing him an aubergine T-shirt, in pima cotton, which feels like angel dust. Riding home I thought of Dante's nine circles of hell. And paper-pale Joe in his sister's dress.

The difference between art and art history is that one does it and the other talks about it, and the talk never seems to jibe with the doing.

The final exam I gave the day before Leon left for Rwanda was partial art identification, part essay: a departmental requirement. Did anyone cheat? Is everyone cheating? Breaking the rules to advance in business, in government, in school, in love? The cheaters consider themselves moral citizens, faithful to the ten laws of Moses, the eleventh being, "Thou shalt not get caught." We dodge taxes, steal cable signals, and pad our expense accounts.

I read a distinctly bizarre essay last week in which *Washington Post Book World* critic Jonathan Yardley links the impact of the civil rights movement to the cheating culture. While he deems the civil rights movement "the noblest and most necessary civil protest in U.S. history," he also notes that that particular protest tried to change unconstitutional laws by violating them. "That it succeeded in doing so is one of the great triumphs in American history. But a wholly inadvertent side effect was that millions of people became persuaded that if they didn't like something—not just the law, anything—they were entitled to protest by disobeying or evading it."

In class one afternoon I noticed a student wearing a pair of extraordinary mules with hand inlaid mother-of-pearl heels. A five-hundred-dollar pair of suede Vicinis.
"What is art?" I asked brazenly.
"These!" she said and pointed to her shoes.
When, with my students, I take a stab at defining *art*, I think of Robert Persig's *Zen and the Art of Motorcycle Maintenance*. Persig struggled with how to teach college rhetoric and somehow fell in love with the notion of "quality." What is "quality"? He recognizes it, the students recognize it (that shock of recognition that distinguishes the real thing from the imposter) and being a philosopher by training, desperately tries to define it. For four hundred or so pages!

Persig states that care and quality are external and internal aspects of the same thing. I tell my students what he told his students. "You have to have a sense of what's good, and that is what carries you forward. Don't separate yourself from the work in such a way as to do it wrong." He tries to define the ineffable "quality". The closest he wants to come is "virtue", not unlike *arite* in Greek, meaning "excellence," what in Sanskrit is called *Dharma*, what Socrates called, "The Source of All Things," what Hermes called *Atum*, and what some of us call "God".

"You've got to live right," he says. "You want to know how to paint a perfect painting? It's easy, make yourself perfect and then just paint naturally. That's the way the experts do it. The making of a painting isn't separate from the rest of your existence." He says something like, "If you're an ass the six days of the week you aren't painting, what can you do suddenly on the seventh day to make art?"

I see Leon's face in Keith Haring colors. Is he wearing a mask? Our last night together he spoke in fragments, broken sentences.

When the African sun glowed red and blood smeared the sky. His tears fell like words down his face. Nietzsche believed that the only things below the masks people wear on their faces are more masks. I ask myself: *Why should I believe Nietzsche?*

Read in a scandal sheet published in Europe that Ella Fitzgerald had both legs amputated due to diabetes. I know she will survive—depending on certain conventions to get here and there, the way some of us depend on dreams.

I'm still mulling over what Trent said about liking Dale just for the sex. How can women blame men for being shallow when women copy them? Isn't copying the highest form of flattery? Not that I'm immune, but at least I see the flesh in context of some larger connection.

Dale cut a perfect circle (did he use a calibrated instrument?) in the wishbone of his madras trousers and sans briefs walked down the block to Starbucks, sat himself down under a big green umbrella and spread the love until a rookie from the 2nd District precinct on Idaho Avenue told him he'd have to go home and put on another pair of pants. I'm sure Dale pled innocent. "Gee, officer," I hear him saying, "I didn't realize I had a geometrically perfect hole," and then I see him flying into a tantrum, tearing himself in half like Rumpelstilskin.

Maybe Trent (who mentions marriage every fourth sentence) should make a wardrobe purchase or two from Talbots, that sensible New England women's clothier. I say this because my friend Sarah, a curator at The Hirshhorn, with stupefying no-knife looks, (voted by *Washingtonian Magazine* one of the most beautiful women in town) used to dress in Chanel cat suits and streak her already blond tresses. She literally stopped traffic over Key Bridge. When I last ran into her at Billy Martin's Carriage House in Georgetown, I was stunned. She still looked good, but admitted, "I want to look *wifely*. I've stopped blonding my hair and wear practically no make up—wear linen and not Lycra to attract the marrying kind." I figure this is a ribald idea (with absolutely no justification) that contains a highly contingent truth.

If I could have visited Ella in the hospital, I would have brought her an enormous spray of gladiolas.

I remember years ago asking my mother what she looked for in a man. I had been reading *Psychology Today* and asked her to name five attributes in order of importance. I poised my black felt-tip marker and a notepad. She was singing "The Battle Hymn of the Republic" and tweezing her eyebrows.

"Punctuality," she said, "is very important."

"Punctuality is the most important trait you can come up with?" I asked.

"Certainly not more important that being a good dancer or a good mixer," she replied.

"A mixer?" I asked. "Do you want a man or a cocktail?"

"A man must have presence and be no stranger to the art of conversation," she continued, swabbing her newly arched brows with a Q-tip dipped in witch hazel.

"Catholic. I want a Roman Catholic," she said.

"Catholicism is the anti-Semitism of the intellectuals," I replied, sounding like a parrot.

I called my colleague, George, a professor of medieval studies at American University, and told him I had a new beau named Leon. "Does he have a Ph.D.?" was his first question, "Does he look good on your arm?" was his second. I realized he was validating what he was bringing to the table as a single man, a quarter-of-a-million-dollar diploma, and escort looks.

"George," I said, "Just because you have a Ph.D. doesn't mean you should refer to yourself as 'doctor'."

"Why not?" he answered. "*Arrivistes* do it all the time."

I tell my art students: "Style is a natural result, not an aim."

People ask me why I read the Hollywood tabloids. I tell them what makes celebrity journalism interesting is the universal reverb.

A Mercedes horn has a horrible timbre.

Leon told me the first time he visited Rwanda he found a girl making broth from a leather sandal.

I love Robert Persig. He writes in *Zen and the Art of Motorcycle Maintenance*, "Philosophically, how are you going to teach virtue if you teach the relativity of all ethical ideas? Virtue, if it implies anything at all, implies an ethical absolute. A person whose idea of what is proper varies from day to day can be admired for his broadmindedness but not his virtue."

My college shrink was large, like a piece of Biedermeier furniture.
"You cannot be the chosen and the chooser," she said. "You cannot be both."
"Why not?" I asked. She seemed too keen to be a college staffer. She should have been at Bellevue, somewhere she could be reasonably inspired by bonafide wackos.
"Liz Taylor and Richard Burton chose each other," I said.
She crossed her thick legs. "Hollywood's version of coupling is a romantic political hoax meant to subordinate women and exculpate men."
Did she happen to see Burton in *Cleopatra,* flaring his nostrils, huffing and puffing around Alexandria in a strangely tiny mini toga?
"Both suffer," she continued, "the women, because they fall for this Dionysian propaganda—"
"When a man cries in my presence," I interrupted, "it means he trusts me," I said, cutting her off. (I figure, the reason she became a psychiatrist in the first place was because she felt cut off, and assumed her vagina fertile ground for her own penis.)
She had a rather draconian haircut. I didn't know any more about her. Was she married? What was her husband like? What I did know was someone she studied under studied under someone who studied

under Karen Horney. (K.H. should have nabbed a *nom de plume*. How can anyone named "Horney," writing about sex, be taken seriously as a scholar?)

"Only an unhealthy person opts for a relationship that requires work," my shrink said.

"Maybe some people like a challenge."

"Bullshit," she said.

I reached into my bag for a cigarette

"You shouldn't smoke," she said.

"What, you want to boycott the tobacco farmers?"

She laughed a full-tilt laugh.

"So what's my homework for this week?"

"Remember, Sylvia, anything that happens to you is inevitable only in retrospect."

I want to live simply with quiet complications. I want to release, flow like plasma. I want to lie alone in a motel room in the apex of summer in a vast bed under a starched sheet. I want to feel the air circulating from a big ceiling fan and hear the whirr of the silver blades.

Mercury must be retrograde. Didn't particularly feel like lecturing so I had the class watch an interview with artist Brice Marden on WETA.

Isn't there a fax in Rwanda? My constant thoughts about Leon must revolve around who I want him to be rather than who he is. Or maybe it's who I want to be. He gives me an opportunity to like myself. We imbue our love objects with all sorts of attributes they don't possess so we can remake ourselves. This is a fact not unlike: the nutrients in an egg are in the yolk, or cotton breathes, or Southern Italians are more demonstrably emotional than Northern Italians. The latter is a climate thing. When it's cold people have to preserve their warmth. You also hear it in the accents of people. There's this closed versus open paradigm when it comes to the north-south axis. Listen to Southerners anywhere. Their vowels are buoyant like beach balls on surf.

I was thinking of Lars, my first man. How much he loved me is moot. In the throes of passion he would wail, "I love you! I love you!"

"Really!" I would respond

"I love all women! Cindy, Eva, You, Claudine, Nadine: fantastic!"

I miss my Uncle Ted. He ate raw garlic cloves between shaved slices of rare roast beef and not only bought me comic books but read them to me. For hours. He also had a glass eye. Several in fact. One with the stars and stripes he wore on Independence Day and one that resembled an olive that he would drop in his martini when company came.

He never said as much, but I think of all his nieces and nephews I was Ted's favorite. When my mother could get him to baby-sit, and he lost his voice (from reading comic books) we used to watch anthropology specials on TV.

"There are few intelligent cold-blooded creatures," I remember him saying. "You need hot blood to run a big brain. That is a metabolic fact! Repeat after me," he'd say, and I'd chime in, "hot blood to run a big brain!" I didn't know what "metabolic" meant. It sounded like some diet drink my mother kept in the refrigerator.

Ted taught me to respect the baboons for their self-agency. He would take me to the zoo, and once in the monkey house, let me belt out "This Old Man" to the baboons. Dance, too, blending some of Miss Binda's ballet steps with "Shaft" movements I'd picked up from *Soul Train*. The performance was a bit abstract, but the baboons liked it. They laughed and pointed and slapped their knees. Sometimes I felt like Tarzan, sometimes like Eva Gabor. All of us were participating in a kind of fusion that felt *right*, if one can call a feeling *right*. "If baboons are so much like us," I asked Ted, "why don't we marry them?"

"We do! Your Aunt Elaine is a baboon of the first magnitude," he bellowed, and at that very moment I discovered soul.

I'm thinking of a very bright student who said of another student's work, "I feel manipulated."

"Why?" I asked.

"It's sentimental," she answered.

"What do you mean by 'sentimental'?"

"Trying to evoke emotions that aren't earned," she answered.

And I went home thinking, *If the emotions are earned isn't that still manipulation? Doesn't da Vinci manipulate us with his virtuosity? Isn't art supposed to do just that?*

Uncle Ted died of angina some years ago. I wear his glass eye (the olive) as a pendant on a gold chain around my neck. Not only in this world, but also in the spirit world, a gold chain connects us.

Another strip bar coming to the neighborhood; another way for cheesy businessmen to make money. The women stripping say they feel empowered. How empowering is it to give a bunch of used car salesmen hard-ons? Sex has just become another industry. It's all become so tedious. Why is it a certain class of women can be paid to endure leering men? This racket alienates men and women sexually, capitalizing on their collective loneliness. All the men who are on board, who say these women can't make the kind of money working in an office that they make stripping—Ask them if they'd mind their daughters mounting a pole, her intimate anatomy displayed while drunk men insert bills where they can. Ask them, could they get down with that, and watch as they squirm. If this is how we have gained immeasurably from the sexual revolution both as partners and parents, then I am Jackie Kennedy and little blue men are barbequing on my porch.

My friend Lauren called today. She went to Dartmouth with me, majored in geology, and worked in upper management at Exxon headquarters in neighboring Virginia before she was put on probation pending psychiatric counseling. Lauren comes from Pawhuska, Oklahoma. Her father is a rancher. There were only thirteen people in her eighth grade class. Her stock is Finnish, which might explain her insular air. Not haughty, just more private than most.

She has been married three years to a wiry Australian who has squandered her money investing in venture capital projects that have tanked. Now the two of them have credit card debt up the yin yang (she is the signatory, so the debt is legally hers) and he has disappeared. He calls periodically from points unknown, saying only that he's lobbying for an Aussie firm and about to hit pay dirt. He doesn't like it when we go out for drinks or dinner because he thinks we're hunting for men.

"Simon called and says he's going to kill you," she tells me over the phone.

I am not unconcerned about this but say, "So?"

I want to go with her to Café Milano on Prospect Street, but the last time we went her husband called the restaurant every five minutes asking for his wife. When the staff became fed up with having to battle the crowds to find Lauren, Simon threatened to report the restaurant to the INS and IRS. At that point, the general manager found her, grabbed her arm, snapped, "Follow me," and escorted her outside. "Never come back here," he hissed.

I missed the incident. I was with Juan, a Cuban transplant from Miami, a lawyer. Juan had invited both of us for dinner, but Lauren, in a groove with a young Jordanian she'd met at the bar, declined. She should have hung with us.

So now, my *Milano* partner is, as they say in the shipping world, dry docked. Her loss, because that place is a goldmine for connections, and she is trying to raise $100,000 for a business, selling concept T-shirts to K-Mart. She's actually snagged a few potential investors, but they all want a *quid pro quo* deal and she won't go there.

The last guy to say he would pony up the capitol invited her to Kennebunkport, booked the two of them in adjoining rooms in one of those reverently dilapidated WASP country clubs, promising he would run it by his law firm, as there were always monies available for lucrative ventures. After caviar, truffles, postprandial toasts of Louis XIII, in front of a delicious fire, he moved to score, she parried, and all of a sudden his firm has no money for any projects, period.

"You will not believe what I found, Lauren says over the phone. "Terrible things—on Simon's hard drive."

I am not surprised because her husband has sweaty palms. And sweaty palms are an index of terrible things. She'd already confessed she'd found (also on Simon's hard drive) specific references to someone getting paid several million in hush money for a nuclear waste disposal scam, which contaminated a 500-acre home site in Fairfax County.

"Like what?" I ask.

"Photos of buildings, sculpture, architecture," she says.

"So?"

"Phallic architecture! And babies playing with broken beer bottles and dirty ashtrays. Babies with *binkies!*"

"*Nostalgie de la boue!*" I exclaim. Then she tells me she's throwing all the shoes she owns that aren't Italian down the incinerator.

"Give them to me," I say.

"They are tainted; you don't want them in your house."

"I sure do," I say. "By the way, what are binkies?"

She tells me there is a man inside of her whose job is moving her legs and arms up and down.

"Like a puppeteer?"

"Exactly!" she says.

"Is he friendly?" This is not a trivial question. Albert Einstein, the king of scientific principle, posed the pivotal question, "Is the universe friendly?"

Lauren and I get together the next day. She wears a white diaphanous dress.

"Maybe we should go out, have a good steak somewhere," I venture.

"Sounds good," she says. I pick her up later. She's still wearing the glacier white Goddess number.

"We have reservations at Ruth's Chris," I say. "Are you hungry?"

"Starved."

At dinner I ask her has she heard from Simon, and she says no. But she has been in contact with some of his family. "The dead ones," she says.

"Really, what do they have to say?"

"They don't speak. They draw."

"Are they Aussies too?"

"Circles and squares. They draw circles and squares. Circles mean: good girl! Squares mean: naughty girl!"

I didn't want to make her wrong. It's not fair really. She is living in a world of thought so different from mine, yet, equally real. The food is hot. The waiter disappears into the great existential void.

"The Asians are crafty, very crafty. Their calendars go from left to right. Subterfuge!" she says.

"Eat," I say. "You're too skinny."

Days later Lauren calls me from Oklahoma where she is visiting her parents. She is resting, breathing fresh air, eating beets. She is under the care of a psychiatrist who has prescribed pills she spits out when no one is watching. She sounds vital, as if everything is hunky dory.

"Well, that's all great news," I say, concluding our call. "Keep in touch."

"Sylvia?"

"Yes?"

"Do you know what happened?"

"What?"

"Why this happened."

"Why?"

"Simon was stung by a female alien. You know who?"

"Who?"

"Patsy Cline," she says with pistol-point clarity.

I Fed-Exed her a miraculous medal, and the day after she receives it she calls saying she's pinned it to her brassiere.

"Can God change His mind?" she asks.

"Yes," I say, "Remember the dowager who kept tugging on the hem of Jesus' robe?" Remember He finally said, 'Woman you have not let me alone,' and then proceeded to give her what she wanted."

"What did she want?"

"A pair of *Via Spiga* shoes!" I say, "Joking!—I think she wanted her sight. I think she was blind."

"Oh," she says, and just when I think we might have been cut off, she mentions a Starbucks in downtown Pawhuska.

"Saw Forrest Gump there earlier last week," she says.

"No kidding."

"He looks just like the guy in the movie," she says.

When I teach a studio art class I get asked a lot of questions, but first I ask one of my own: did you choose painting or did painting choose you? It's for *their* benefit I ask the question, not *mine*. Because if they are considering living the life of an artist and can do something else they should. Unless they have no choice.

"What should I paint?" they ask.

"Flowers or fruit; you choose." They look alarmed. "My point is you don't need layered narratives or imaginary monsters. Keep it simple, and get to the 'nut' of things. The difference between Pissarro, who was capable, and Van Gogh, who was genius, is that Van Gogh obsessed for the *yellowness* of yellow in a lemon, for the *shabbiness* of shabby in a shoe."

They tell me they don't understand art criticism, and I tell them I don't understand it either. It seems abstruse, enough pseudo-academic crap to fertilize all the poppies in Turkey.

Before Leon, there was Greg, and if that relationship weren't so sad it would have been hilarious. I met Greg at Café Milano, especially popular (with the Cabinet, Congress and capricious beauties) on Thursday nights. Greg was soft spoken, simple (a major plus), easy on the eyes (tall, lean, youthful), interested in me, and unattached (another plus, given the profusion of *MBAs:* "Married But Available," on the circuit).

His job was a bit of a mystery. He said he owned five Dominos store franchises, later three, but after we started dating, I'd visit him at the same Dominos every time where he made subs and pizzas. No big deal what he did for a living. I was just confused.

Greg was working out some adolescent script. We'd been dating for a month, and one evening when we were to get together, he didn't show. Turned out he was spray-painting *Surrender Dorothy* (from *The Wizard of Oz*) on a trellis above Interstate 495.

He also lived in a rooming house that had been condemned for radon poisoning. Greg was 45.

One day I told him I'd purchased tickets to *The Vagina Monologues*.

"The Vergina Monologues?" he asked.

"Spell *vagina,*" I said.

"V-E-R-G-I-N-A," he replied. (*Might as well call them "The Virginia Monologues",* I thought.)

I don't want to be a slave to my desires, but I felt Greg and I shared something more than just desire. We had been dating six weeks, and though we were attracted to one another, no physical closeness of any consequence had developed.

"What's up?" I finally asked. He had a plethora of explanations. "I didn't think you were ready," was one. Flatulence was another. Apparently flatulence had disturbed his former girlfriend. Then he said my apartment was too hot. Finally he confessed it was his prostate.

"Is it an enlarged?" I asked.

"They're not sure. I have a problem when I sleep on my side," he said demurely. "Gas."

He sent me roses the color of dawn with a note penned on a scrap piece of paper, apologizing in advance for his lack of sexual p-r-o-r-w-e-s-s.

When he called I thanked him.

"You're so welcome," he said. He was quiet for a moment and then said he had something to tell me.

"What is it?" I asked. He hesitated. I could feel what he wanted to say was difficult for him. Finally he blurted it out.

"I can't date a girl who smokes," he said.

"Greg, when you met me I was smoking."

"I thought I could handle it; but the other night when we kissed, I wanted to leave."

I love this sort of thing, I thought. *It's so paradigmatic.*

Not long after, we were dining *alfresco* on the edge the Potomac River and happened on some interesting sandals in a waterfront store.

"Would you wear those?" I asked.

"Sure, if I didn't have a foot fungus," he said.

"I thought you were an *homme de gout*! A man of taste!" I said. "Why would you share that with me at this moment?"

He could limbo. He was a good listener. He never raised his voice, and he treated me to many succulent dinners. He looked every bit as good as Jimmy Smits, and though he'd warned me of his performance issues, it didn't seem to be that big a deal.

"You have a Colgate smile," I told him one Sunday afternoon after we had toured the National Cathedral gardens.

"These are false," he chimed, "I have twenty false teeth. Missing teeth run in my family. My twin sister. We both have twenty missing teeth." His porcelain veneers gleamed.

It must have been after The Stones' concert at the MCI Center when I noticed a prescription bottle filled with pills on his car dash.

"What's this?" I asked. I couldn't read the label. Moisture had smeared the words.

"Medicine," he said.

"What for?"

"O this rash I get on my tailbone from doing sit ups on a towel in the sauna."

"Really," I paused. "So why didn't the doctor give you some topical ointment instead of pills?"

"Don't know."

"Well, what is it? Warts? Impetigo? Ringworm? You can get impetigo from a dirty sauna."

"I use a towel."

"And?"

"Doctor says it will come and go."

"It is herpes?"

"No."

"All these problems, all this seamy hoopla," I cried.

Mentally, I ran through the list. The sexual dysfunction, combined with the prostate problem, the gastrointestinal disorder, false teeth, rash on his buttocks, and foot fungus. Too *Jerry Springer* for me! Whom the gods want to destroy they first make ridiculous. But what god would want to destroy Greg? He was a sweetheart, and despite all his flaws, still winsome to me.

"Why are you with this guy?" my friend Steven, an attorney for the Justice Department, asked. "Has he been married before?"

"He says his ex-wife, whom he met in college, was voted *best body on the beach* in a Playboy poll, and that she was invited to lunch with the President of The United States because her SAT scores were so high."

"Which president? Clinton?" Steven asked.

"I don't know which president, Steven."

"And," I continued, "that her rich aunt funded the construction of the National Presbyterian Church."

"He sounds like a walking petri dish."

"At least he's not Italian."

"What wrong with Italians?"

"Italian men! Didn't you read Shelly Winters' autobiography about her marriage to Vittorio Gassman?"

Greg's and my love life continued but did not improve. So one evening, when he appeared relaxed, and Sarah Vaughn scatted on a CD, I asked him if he was attracted to me.

"You know I am."

As delicately as possible I asked what was going on.

"It's not that you are not desirable," he began. I nodded, giving him my full attention. "But—I have this condition I have never told you about."

I thought, *This dog ain't huntin'*, meaning me. I was done.

To make a long story short, he said he had a painful sphincter and that he had been to a score of colonoscopists, none of who could agree on a diagnosis. He'd purchased an inflatable cushion designed with a hole in the center (a donut), so he could sit with temporary relief. He toted the donut around.

"My mother has the same problem," he said.

"Too many salted peanuts," I said, quoting Mickey Spillane.

He glared at me.

"It hurts you to lie down too?" I asked.

"The only relief I get comes when I walk around."

I thought, *What a Borgia-like drama.* I said, "I think this has to do with the engine in your Toyota Land Cruiser."

The Toyota he'd been driving for seven years was built with the engine right under the seat, and it got very hot. When I had driven with him to Canada for that snack convention he'd sat on that seat for hours. "How can any *sentient being* sit for sixteen hours with a hot engine right under his bum?" I'd asked.

I adjusted the volume on the Sarah Vaughn CD. "Does your mother drive a Toyota?" I asked.

"I need to walk around," he answered.

"You called me 'Angel' the other day. No man has ever called me 'Angel'. 'Devil', yes, 'Angel,' no."

He continued walking around.

"I'm embarrassed to tell you," he began.

"Don't be shy," I said.

He hedged.

"Just tell me, please?"

He inhaled and exhaled deeply.

"What's wrong sweetheart?" And then, with the emotional anguish of *Antigone*, Greg said, "I cannot make love because I am in pain."

Behind his face in the bay window I saw the gloss of a forbidding moon. We held each other in its shadow. I realize this is the intimacy, almost larval, that I craved.

I gathered these ailments were intended to push me away. But what was wrong with me? Was his pain in his rectum or his heart? Maybe his heart ached because he was afraid of intimacy. So I went to my confessor, who happens to be a Jesuit from India, an extremely kind man named Father Joy, who grew up with no running water or septic system in a poor village south of Maharashtra.

"Is he a street person?" Father Joy asked.

"I don't think so, Father Joy," I said.

"He sounds like a street person," Father Joy replied.

Then Greg showed up at the rectory with an extra large pepperoni pie, and Father Joy never referred to Greg that way again.

I think one of the cardinal problems with Greg was that he did not remember much. What he did, what he said, and his attempts at reconstructing either, made him sound like a liar. The details were inconsistent, dramatis personae interchangeable, and plots eliminated or created for better or worse. I understand most men have selective memories (evolution-wise, it's a survival skill) but Greg's memory lapses did not work to his advantage. I tried to piece the puzzle together. He had been born three months premature, one pound, an identical twin. No one had informed his mother she was carrying twins. The obstetrician who delivered his twin sister was in his car in the parking lot when Greg swam through the birth canal. I think his last minute birth, coupled with gestation trauma (no one knew he existed! Plus his mother smoked Cigarillos) impacted his psycho-sexual-physical self. The sanguine thing was he didn't imagine himself compromised! He reminded me of the diva Maria Callas. She had such an amplified self-concept. Once after performing at *La Scala* in Milan, the audience, unhappy with her singing, threw tomatoes on the stage. She could not imagine herself the target of tossed tomatoes. *She thought they were roses*!

I asked Greg about his buddies.

"They all take sex enhancers," he said.

"Greg, you take sex enhancers."

"We are *Titans*!" he chanted, "Imperial, fine-tuned machines!" (*Titans*! What did he know about mythology?)

I think structural abnormalities in the frontal cortex of his brain developed in utero. Whatever cell mass is associated with language/memory. One time he meant to use the expression *blow a gasket* and said instead, *blow a casket*.

"They bury people in a casket," I reminded him.

It become clear he'd lost the passion. He would forget to call and when he did call, sounded inert. "You should be in a casket. Dating you is like dating a cadaver," I wanted to say, "and your pizza has so very little cheese. I'm embarrassed for you! So cheap!"

My friend Rosa says, "Sylvia, stop dating these little people. You're too sophisticated to be dating a fast-food guy. It's like Sharon Stone dating Opie Taylor. You're just lonely," she continues. "Anyone will tell you nature abhors a vacuum." She sighs then asks, "Do you feel used?"

"Am I the type of woman who would let a man use me?"

"We all use one another. That's what we call love."

"That's refreshing," I say.

"You can't have him," she says.

"Why?" I ask.

"If you could have him you wouldn't love him. Sylvia, you don't want to marry this guy."

"True. Even if he did love me."

"Then what is the problem? It's a game with you, Sylvia. You just want to win."
"If I want to win so badly, why am I losing?"
"Maybe you want to lose. In the bone you want to lose."
"What do you mean, 'in the bone'?"
"Maybe you pick people who can't love you."
"Wait a minute," I said; "I'm confused. In the bone, do I want to win, or do I want to lose?"

Was I a good girlfriend? Grade-wise I'd given myself an A- /B+. I'd driven him to Montreal for that snack convention, and I hate long car rides (but I do love to snack). I tried to empathize with his array of maladies. I tried to be cheerful.
"We should communicate more when we're naked," he said once.
"Why do we have to be naked to communicate?" I answered.

"Why do you think I like you?" I remember asking him.
"Because I am adventurous. You'd never slept under the stars, and you had that adventure with me," he said.
Wow, I thought, *Words mean so many things to so many people. "Adventurous" to me means betting your mortgage on a double-or-nothing roulette spin. Anybody can sleep in a sleeping bag. The inexorable question was, "What have you risked?"*

"I don't like Las Vegas," I told him once.
"Las Vegas has its own weather system," he said.
"I still don't like it," I replied.

"You know what I like most about your body?"
"What?"
"Your ribcage," he said.
Bug off, I thought. *If you want to see a ribcage go to The Smithsonian Museum of Natural History and check out the brontosaurus skeletons.*

I ran into him at Starbucks on New Mexico Avenue months after we had split. I was seated in a purple velvet armchair, composing a poem on a napkin.

"You look good," I said.

"So do you," he answered. "Better naked."

I smiled, flattered and disgusted at the same time. Who says you can't experience two emotions at once?

"Writing your to-do list?"

"A poem," I answered. I bit into my *biscotto*.

"Really," he said, "You have time to write poetry?"

"Listen." I began:

The ginger-ale blond, tall as a silo, spoke to the man on the tractor. "They are lost," she said, as she glanced toward the herd of nine, the tails of the thin deer flashing like crosses in the sun.

"You are so deep," he said.

"It's just an image," I said. "How about this one? I pulled another napkin from my pile and read:

I was adopted and when I turned thirty began to look for my mother. At forty, after a Promethean search, I found her, invited her over for pot roast. 'That is a very pretty television,' she said, eyeing my 27-inch Hitachi. 'Would you like it?' I asked. 'Yes, I would,' she answered. We loaded it into her Pontiac, and I never heard from her again.

I began to laugh before I finished reading because I think this is hilarious. I laughed so hard I spilled my triple espresso. "So what's new with you?" I asked.

"All five franchises, going great. Thinking of selling a couple for north of a million."

"Do it!" I said.

He looked out the store's fog-clotted window. His smile waned.

"I just got back from Georgetown Hospital. Seems I have an infection in my left testicle." He took the prescription out of his pocket and waved it in my face like a tiny party favor.

I felt sorry for his testicle problem and for the fact we were finally burying our dead child. That's what it felt like. The relationship had expired.

Months later I forgave myself. For getting involved with him in the first place, and, once involved, not being able to manage the relationship or at least understand Greg's problems were too serious for me to fix.

I went to see Reverend Justinian today, a clairvoyant I consult now and again.

Before I started to date Greg, the Reverend, in a vision, saw me prostrate in a field of tomatoes. Later I realized the tomatoes were pizza ingredients and that the Reverend was exercising his symbolic prescience as usual.

"I met a man named Leon," I said this time. "Do you see our getting married?"

He closed his eyes and then with his airborne forefinger drew the imaginary border of a square.

"I see you in a pink suit with a man. I think it's you, but your back is to me: his too. You are in a church, and it looks like a wedding."

"My wedding?"

He nodded.

"How do I look?"

"Let me turn you around," he said. With his thumb and forefinger he manipulated an imaginary image of me. "You're smiling."

"Is *he*?"

He turned my future husband around in the air. "He's sweating," Reverend said.

"It must be hot in the church."

"No, he's nervous. You are patting him on the shoulder, assuring him everything will be okay."

Took the Reverend to lunch at an all-you-can eat diner with chicken and dumplings, the best pulled pork, fresh kale, and piping hot cheese grits, plus liquor! The Reverend, recuperating from a gallbladder operation (the surgeon nicked something he shouldn't have) has a tube from his stomach connected to a drip bag.

Psychics have a hard time foreseeing their own future.

Regarding my future, the disconcerting fact remains: Whatever "is set up for me," i.e., what the Reverend *sees*, is subject to change. He explained, "The vibration may change." Last visit, he told me I was going to paint Motion Picture Association of America's President Jack Valenti's Yorkie. Someone from Valenti's office did contact me, but ultimately the MPAA chose another portrait artist. So from what I gather, what the Reverend *sees* is a distinct possibility taking shape. But as it can change, what is the point?

Pigeons are roosting in my apartment. I opened all the windows in my home because I had started a small fire from meat I was cooking! I don't have screens because the windows in my apartment are protected by some historical society. Because the building is an architectural landmark, and the window fittings are old (probably calcified) I have to formally petition a board of directors for screens.

My mother calls, as she does every couple of months, and I tell her about the pigeons.

"My God," she screams, "don't you know they carry disease?"

I say, "Mother, pigeons are the lepers of the bird world. Did that stop Father Damian living in the leper colonies? Would I not invite someone diagnosed with a fatal disease to be a guest in my home? May God strike me dead if I would ever discriminate against *any* living being because he was sick."

Before Greg there was Mike. Mike always wore Ray-Bans.

"Who do you think you are," I asked him, "Admiral Perry?" (Admiral Perry must have worn sunglasses. The arctic ice increases the sun's glare exponentially.)

"I wear sunglasses because I'm photo phobic."
"You fear light?"
I think he feared enlightenment. He confided in me, months after we stopped dating, that he took casual sex very seriously. He also admitted that after he made love to a woman, he wished she were dead. There is no such thing as casual sex, only casualties.

I was in limerance, with Michael, stage A of mating, that crush thing. Whoever isolates the neurotransmitters produced in the limerant stage will win a Nobel. It will be a discovery as important as insulin. It will reduce crime. Think what percentage of crimes committed are crimes of passion.

Michael and I did not last long. "I prefer Asian women with slanty eyes and small breasts," he admitted one evening, in rhythmic bass tones that suggested the easy grasp on power he'd held most of his life.

I once asked this man I'd met at a Corcoran fund-raiser what he did. I had a hunch he taught at their school of art. "I'm a photographer," he answered. "I solve problems with light."

And I thought, *What kind of aesthetic paganism is this? Has he no faith in the unknown? That guiding force that takes charge when we allow it? Furthermore, isn't art not so much about solving problems but presenting them? Wasn't art about dignifying the mystery of all that is?*

My shrink once said, "Sylvia, you don't want a boyfriend. You want a slave."

"That's ridiculous," I said, and then considered it.

I once invited the gardener and the janitor from the college to my home. The gardener confessed while I was baking a wheel of Brie, that his mother had advised him not to let his "wee-wee" make a "slave" of him.

"Well, have you?"
"Have I what?"
"Have you let your wee-wee make a slave out of you?"

"*Never*," he replied. "It was *never* a wee-wee."

I met Cathy at Starbucks, where it seems I meet all my unorthodox friends. I told her I liked her diamond earrings, and she immediately confessed they were not real.

"Why mention that?" I asked.

"So no one will steal them," she answered. She told me about her Nigerian boyfriend, "whose hygiene is impeccable."

"He comes home everyday at five o'clock," she said. "He is the most dedicated man."

"That's great!"

She adds, "His wife lives in Nigeria."

I nod my head in rapt attention. Cathy is a white, educated, woman of size, with thick red hair. She had a big-wheel job but now lives on food stamps, which she explained are not really stamps, but a kind of ATM card you slide at the register at any grocer.

"I needed a break from corporate culture," she confessed. Cathy has no phone, no television, radio, or car.

"He wants to take me to Nigeria," she says.

"That would be a fascinating trip," I respond.

"Why would I want to go to a dirty place like that?" she asks me, as if I'm a complete screwball.

"Well, yes," I say, "especially with the wife being there."

I invite Cathy for dinner *chez-moi*, because she has no money to dine out and obviously enjoys eating. This way I can fix her a tasty meal.

"Tell me your favorite dish," I say, "and I will create it for you!"

She beams.

"And after dinner we can go to Sharper Image, in Tyson's Corner Mall, and relax on the battery-powered massaging recliners!" she says, "for free!"

"Sounds like a plan!" I reply.

As she is leaving I mention, "Please feel free to bring your Nigerian boyfriend." She tells me he parades nude around their apartment. And that he wears hand-tooled genital jewelry.

MEN and WOMEN, what Timothy Leary called *the most important drama in the human experience.* MY NOTES:

What about the token males who infiltrated the Seven Sister colleges when those colleges became co-ed? What type of guy would want to go to an all girls' school? An all out red-blooded male? One would think. It turns out, the men who entered Vassar, Smith, Holyoke etc. were considered somewhat feminine while the women who entered traditional men's schools e.g. Dartmouth, Yale, Princeton, were considered either lucky, or competent.

What do women want? Power, equal wages, sexual predatory rights? How much more aggressive can we get? We're out-alpha-ing the men, so the men push the pedal even further. I meet my girlfriend at Morton's bar for a drink. A well-dressed lobbyist with nineteenth century diction introduces himself and in the next fifteen minutes asks us if we use vibrators. This seems normal cocktail chat these days. Once women began to talk freely about their anatomy/sexual appetites, men hopped on the bandwagon. Is this emancipation? There is no greater prison than feeling trapped in a dialogue you find sexually offensive. If you exit the conversation these days, you're labeled a prude. But the truth is, we women fashioned a niche for men to indulge their libidos and not be censured socially for it. Of course many men would love to reference sex in the first few minutes of conversation with a woman whom they found attractive. Now many do. We gave them permission.

A male acquaintance asked me where he could meet beautiful women. I told him to loiter around the cosmetic department at Saks Fifth Avenue. So he did until Security picked him up. Ha!

Katherine Hepburn once said you can fall in love with an old shoe if it is around long enough.

My girlfriend married a younger man, who asked her, "Do you think we are soul mates?"

She said, "No."

"Was I *ever* your soul mate?" he asked.

"No," she said, "but who cares? I love you, and that's what matters."

I remarked to a male acquaintance that men commit suicide at four times the rate of women.

"At some level that means men are not women and nothing more," he said.

"Which level is that?" I asked.

Are men less equipped to handle their or any one else's emotions because they are less affiliative by nature? Men are taught not to air their personal issues. Actually, why can't we deduce that because men kill themselves at four times the rate females do, that men are emotionally inferior to women?

Sometimes I wonder why more men don't bitch about all the men-bashing that has become the national pastime.

What about androgenic alopecia a.k.a. baldness? Men's nemesis. And yet how would Michael Jordan look with a full head of hair?

They've apparently done it!

Isolated the neurotransmitter *phenylethylamine*. The love drug! Lasts eighteen months to three years before the brain stops producing it or reacting to it.

My friend Bill, who belongs to Burning Tree, the most exclusive golf club in the Washington area, says that nude, he has shaken hands (in the club's locker room) with the following (also nude) presidents: Eisenhower, Ford, Carter, Kennedy, and Johnson.

"Did you look into their eyes when you shook hands or is there a silent code whereby you assess each other on another, more manly level?"

When relationships end, women mourn, men replace.

Why do men make grunting noises lifting weights at the gym?

The green spoon worm's idea of foreplay is inhaling her mate. Females in more than eighty species have been caught eating their lovers before, during, or after coitus. What possibly could be the evolutionary point of that?

Olivia de Havilland's advice to women, "Never go Dutch on a date. The more men spend on you, the more they value you." I think the more we pay for something, whether in money, effort, or time, the more valuable it becomes.

Which candidate denounced the concept of nation building during a presidential election debate? Whoever, said that U.S. military intervention in foreign countries had to meet three criteria. The mission had to be in our vital interest. It had to be clear. And the exit strategy had to be obvious. I thought at the time, *Salient dating advice*.

When I first started teaching at Mount Vernon on Foxhall Road, I dated a man named Tom. He shared your run of the beltway garden apartment with two male roomies. Tom himself was thirty-five, a little old for this arrangement if you ask me. (Truth is, I would have fallen for him if he lived in a teepee.) He'd taken the basement bedroom, probably because it was the cheapest (he didn't make much money) and painted it pale yellow. *Sunlight* was the name of the shade, he informed me. Odd, because the *last* thing that room looked was sunlit. His bedroom closet, made from congruent bamboo slats, was open. I noticed a pair of sunlit trousers. Who wore these besides Hilton Head Island golfers and 1970 Vanderbilt preppies? Another pair, made of patchwork squares, looked like a bedspread. "That's my stuff," he said proudly. He reveled in this primitive description of what he owned, pointing to his clothes like an aborigine proud of his chickens. I didn't glimpse any belts embroidered with waterfowl, fashion he hadn't been exposed to, given his modest background. His father sold furniture. His mother was as a nurse. An 8 x 1O photo of his mother and Salvadoran half sister, shot against a cartoon blue background, hung on his wall.

This is the room we slept in. In a wide bed he would find me at intervals during the night. Intervals are the spaces between tones that make music. Down deep, I wanted to hang onto him as you do the last note in a hymn, when the organ swells and you cry with joy because you're with God and not Darth Vader.

Got a call today from an acquaintance I met at Starbucks last summer when she was visiting D.C. She was admitted two days ago to Georgetown Hospital's psychiatric ward. Stunning girl, early twenties, father an oil tycoon from Venezuela. He'd bought her a black Mercedes to tool around in on her vacation. By fall, she'd found a sexy U.S. reprobate (prison record) turned clean. As we all know, desire can preclude good judgment: see Clinton. Tatiana married him and immediately conceived.

Soon the husband started beating her up.

Since Tatiana's father never endorsed the marriage, Papa stopped the cash flow, and to her credit, Tatiana went to work right away cleaning houses (something she could do without work papers). She would drive up in her Benz, clean four houses a day, and clear three hundred dollars. She worked until she became too big to lug a vacuum around. She both wanted and had the baby. From what I understand, the husband is still up to no good. He's nabbed a couple of assault charges gleaned from a bar brawl and has been delinquent in paternity support. She is living alone, still cleaning houses, and her mother, divorced from Tatiana's father, is caring for the baby boy in Venezuela. Layer upon layer of problems (think of building a lasagna) ensued for Tatiana. The fact she missed her infant son, the fact she'd married a loser, the fact that daycare (if she brought the son to the States) would run two hundred a week, and that rent (Washington is off the charts) was costing her thirteen hundred dollars a month for a one-bedroom in a decent neighborhood. Now that she was legal she had to pay taxes, and since she had expanded her cleaning business, had also to supervise a group of maids who, on occasion, stole.

I went to see her in the hospital, brought her the latest *Vogue*, a Nokia radio, and a carton of Marlboro Lights.

The door to the ward on the 4th floor of Georgetown University Hospital was locked. A video camera scanned me (I look non-threatening), and I was buzzed in. A man I met at Café Milano, who had spent four years in the seminary before working in a mental ward, told me that people in a ward who either pretend they are Jesus or hear Him are the most dangerous, the most likely to harm themselves and/or others. "The devil's modus operandi," I remember saying to him, "The king of lies, the author of confusion. What a *canny* way to discredit Jesus!"

Well no one in the ward was talking about Jesus. One homeless man who had faked a suicide attempt so he could be given a private room, clean sheets, and hot water, shuffled out of the community room, and seeing Tatiana and I, headed to the smoker (patients could smoke only on the hour in this tiny room), and asked if I had an extra cigarette.

"Help yourself," I said, offering him my pack. Another man yelled from the community room. "Tell her you ain't even got an address!"

"I don't need an address," the homeless man said. "Look at this body! One hundred thirty pounds of raw tiger meat!" He lifted up his shirt. I thought of the lost wisdom of the Pharaohs, a 3000 year old scroll titled *The Hermetica* that maintains the gods ensure that an individual's frame is fashioned in conformity with his soul, seeing to it that lively souls have lively bodies, sluggish souls have sluggish bodies, powerful souls have powerful bodies, and so on. At this point, the shirt-lifter tells the angry man, "You're one to talk; you live in public housing!"

His riled-up foe answers, "The President of the United States lives in public housing!"

Then a rather slim lady seated in the community room, who up until now has said nothing, yells, "Fools! You can have trash in the White House and class in the projects!"

In an instant, a fifty-something woman with gray, cotton-candy hair, apparently woken from the racket, comes out of her room, looks me straight in the eye and says, "I could deal with this shit if I'd smoked a couple of grams of black-tar heroine."

What keeps people crazy is the animosity of others toward them. Humans sense fear and hostility in others. And it ricochets. Break the cycle. Be kind to the mentally deranged.

"I need to be circumcised," the slim lady says solemnly. "All I think of is f——ing."

"Content yourself with being a lover of wisdom and seeker of truth," I say, not to be funny, but to plant a seed.

"I am woman; hear me roar," she sings.

This is a sort of a boutique ward I figure, no real gonzos, no straight jackets or padded cells. Tatiana wanted me to bring diet pills (she's a size 4), and I said no because even *I* know her psychiatrists would veto phentermine with all she's taking right now.

"You might get suicidal," I said, and then realized she'd been admitted for just that reason. I tell Tatiana I want to meet the hoarder. (Excessive collecting is a pathology.) What drug cures that? (I love psychopharmacology.) Is there a trichotillomaniac in the house? Trichotillomaniacs have a nervous habit of pulling out their hair, eyebrows, eyelashes. If you ask me, this is a simple disease to explain. The T's want to erase themselves. They symbolically begin by literally denuding themselves. It's like nail biting, only worse.

I may go nuts one day, and if I do (God says, "Make your requests known") I want a Negro nanny filled with the love of Jesus to live with me in my house (no mental hospitals, please) and be the mother I lost.

I think most nutty people suffer from a lack of love. Either for themselves or for others. We shouldn't be so punishing. *Who's to say the water lilies in Monet's paintings might not actually be flying saucers?*

Many Christians say God never gives anyone more than he can handle. Explain suicide then, I say. They generally don't have an answer, but I do.

When you're in *connect* with God, suicide is not an option. Is there any classic Western or Eastern traditional religion that *actually* condones suicide? The respect you accord Him for creating you is living your life. But, and here comes the hairy part, if God loves all of us equally, why wouldn't He try to save the non-believers from annihilating themselves? Let's face it; people don't usually say, "I'm so happy I'm going to stick my head in an oven." People who commit suicide are usually despairing. If God does not come to the rescue of despairing individuals it's only because they've shut Him out. God offers His grace, what it takes to handle whatever situation, and those bent on suicide say, "No." He doesn't force Himself on you. God's not a gatecrasher. He respects your free will. Of course, there are times He comes to your rescue anonymously. People who think they are merely lucky are really getting gifts from God with no card.

Some posit, If He knows what I need why doesn't He just give it to me? Why must I ask? The reason He wants to be asked is because He wants a communion with you.

I tell my students to respect their viewers, just as I think an author should respect his readers. I once took a master studio art class at NYU and was pressed for my opinion on some bad art. I said I felt as if I'd been invited to a dinner party and served junk food.

Have you seen Dr. Kevorkian's art? Worse yet. Looking at it, you feel as if someone is trying to poison you. It's hopeless, bleak, and abysmal. Maybe he sees the world that way, but if what the doctor feels he is doing is good, why aren't his paintings better? Nobel Laureate Elie Wiesel says literature, real literature, has an ethical dimension. You can understand this when you take into account the fact he was prisoner at Buchenwald. What is ethical is enormously important for him, given the unethical dimension of what he experienced. So does that make him wrong about literature? You don't have to have survived the Nazis to value what is good in art and in life.

If the practice of Zen Buddhism condones emotional detachment, how can one love God with all his heart?

In the Old Testament, the Israelites were given their daily ration of manna and quail. Some tried to stockpile the food for future use, and it spoiled. Trust in God's provision. He is not going to give you today what you need tomorrow. How else could we learn to trust in Him?

My friend, a gemologist, viewed a twenty-carat diamond in Boston's Academy of Science and wept. Maybe he wept because the diamond is flawless, and he is not.

Tearing up photographs of people is a form of homicide. No?

An ad for a Spanish film reads, "*Una historia de amor y dolor*"— no American movie promo would read, "*y de dolor*". Americans have become too comfortable with the absence of pain. I can't wait to read a movie review that warns in fine print: "Contains sad anecdotes and emotional content."

Elie Wiesel wrote a book in which one man asks another why he cried when he prayed. The second man said he didn't know. Then the first man asked the second why he prayed at all. "I don't know," the second man replied, frustrated because he didn't have an answer, frustrated because he didn't realize he may have been learning more looking for the answer than finding it.

In *Sweet Bird of Youth*, Tennessee Williams writes:

...the great difference between people in this world is not between rich and poor or the good and evil, the biggest difference in this world is between the ones that had or have pleasure in love and those that haven't and hadn't any pleasure in love, but just watched it....The spectators and the performers. I don't mean just ordinary pleasure or the kind you can buy. I mean great pleasure. Pleasure without peer.

When I find a worm struggling on the sidewalk I relocate him to the soil to rest. I cover him with a green leaf moistened with water I keep in a bottle in my car. Suppose God had made us worms? Worms cling to life as much as we do.

How do you serve? It's easy to write a check, tax deduct it, show up at the fund-raiser for the latest chic disease, and get quoted in a society column. It's easy to spend Thanksgiving at a soup kitchen when you've ignored your own brother's phone calls. It's easy to quit alcohol or stop bleaching your hair when you're pregnant because it's bad for the baby. But how bad for the baby is it when its vacuumed from the womb and tossed in a trash can because Mommy couldn't be bothered with contraception?

Why are people breeding pedigreed dogs when hundreds of thousands of beautiful mutts are being euthanized in our animal shelters daily? If people are so gung-ho on pure lineage (and why should it begin and end with dogs?) we risk the genetically superior mentality that fueled the Second World War, an even larger genocide. The way I see it, we are all connected. Someone once asked me, "Is Jesus right? Is his message right?"

"Read the parables," I say. "You decide whom you want to model. You decide how you want to live."

I remember asking my Uncle Ted how sure was his faith. In words as smooth as stones, he answered, "I live the questions."

You decide if you have the character to live the questions. The Buddhists call this living, "Right action, the eight-fold path."

When someone says, "Nothing good comes easy," I'm inclined to agree.

Maybe that great pleasure Tennessee Williams refers to comes as a reward for something else, all that effort a girl spends dating frogs in search of a prince, being nice to guys with acne and brown shoes because you don't want to hurt their feelings.

A colleague says, "Hey, I painted that painting in three hours, and it won a juried prize!"

And I say, "How many years was that painting in pre-production? How many years were you subconsciously collecting data to make that painting?" I've always said, premier musical albums are usually the best because the musician has been preparing his whole life for that debut.

A friend says to me, "How easy is it to be generous?"

And I ask him, "Were you born generous? What event in your life taught you that you are only worth what you give away? Was that lesson easy?"

Maybe something is easy for you because your parents (or their parents) bore its difficulty—and you are getting the reward for their sacrifice. I am convinced happiness is an investment that involves sacrifice.

Met a man at Nathan's (the granddaddy of saloons on Wisconsin Avenue and M Street) who, through manual labor, sent three daughters to college. The joy that he experienced when they walked on stage to receive their diplomas was supreme.

Something may seem effortless. The Bible reads, "Consider the lilies of the field, they neither toil nor spin, but even Solomon, in all his glory, is not arrayed like one of these." I watch the lilies, spellbound by their beauty, but acquiring that appreciation came by way of tremendous longing.

Today around 5:00 p.m., on my way home from yoga, I was startled by what I heard. I looked up in the trees and saw a cardinal. His lipstick-red body, a few ounces in weight, hardly the mass of a child's slipper, let alone a two-hundred-pound soprano, produced a sound so clean and round, so absolute. He'd sing and then he'd stop, giving me time to assimilate his choice of notes and their length before beginning his next musical phrase. I was knocked out by the notion that this bird—via some metaphysical scheduling—had agreed to this private recital. My listening was as fierce as his singing.

Pablo Neruda remembers a connection he made when he was a child, an exchange of small gifts, a pinecone and a faded toy sheep, with a boy about his own age, a stranger he never saw again. Neruda writes:

> *That exchange brought home to me for the first time a precious idea: that all humanity is somehow together...this is the great lesson I learned in my childhood, in the backyard of a lonely house. Maybe it was nothing but a game two boys, who didn't know each other played, two boys who wanted to pass to the other some good things in life. Yet maybe this small and mysterious exchange of gifts remained inside me also, deep and indestructible, giving my poetry light.*

If I could only bring my students back to the place where, when they were children, they created free, unencumbered, paintings; where there was no divide between who they were and what they painted.

I tell them true poetry communicates before it is understood. I tell them if I have to try to understand their painting, what went wrong? I tell them there is such a thing as emotional logic.

Had a fabulous bowl of *Mussels Saint Nazaire* at the Peacock Café in Georgetown last week. Was seated by myself at the bar, and when I suggested to the bartender that I might have a second bowl (this was my dinner), he asked me, "Are you sure?"

I thought about it for a few seconds then said, no, I wasn't sure. Only because my appreciation for the experience would have been compromised. One bowl was perfect. Any more would have subtracted from the experience. Food tastes better when one is hungry. Of course there is the element of surprise (something also endemic to art). I was surprised how delicious that first bowl of mussels was. The second bowl would not have surprised me.

Those few measures of song. When you paint, don't over produce. You will know when to stop. There is action and rest. Is prayer action or rest? The Bible reads, "Pray without ceasing." Perhaps The Bible is talking of breathing. Why not make your breath a prayer? Because at the bottom of each breath is a hollow to be filled.

Those months while I was looking for a teaching post, I took a job as a receptionist in northern Virginia. I liked the low-stress, meeting-greeting thing. What I didn't like was the sloppiness of my supervisors, which had spread like mold from the top ranks down. I would get phone lists that hadn't been updated for months, employees' names misspelled. Abusing privilege was another problem. One VP who hired his wife and her girlfriends to dress up as pilgrims (go figure, maybe it was supposed to be Dickensian) and sing at the Christmas party, billed the company the equivalent of his daughter's college tuition, while firing a payroll-processing father of six two days before he was to receive his Christmas bonus. This payroll processor had accused his boss of micro-managing and was summarily fired for insubordination. Virginia is an *at will* state, so this worker (not being of color, an exotic religion, or particularly old), was essentially toast.

Was everyone in that office on Demerol or did they just look that way? Plants were dying everywhere. I'm convinced there is a one-to-one correlation between those who don't water their plants and those who can't be bothered to return voice mail. One lady, confined in her cubicle, sold Siamese fighting fish, prodding customers to starve them to make them nastier. Can you imagine? Munchausen's by Proxy invades the aquatic world. I have a thing for fish. Sea life is a potent symbol of the ancient force that dignifies even the most attenuated lives. Why was she exempt? Irony of ironies: her last name was *Water*.

When Hassidism was first introduced in Poland in the 1600s, the prevailing litmus test that determined a good Jew was not what he knew but what he felt. Provided our feelings reflect the value of the human condition, shouldn't that litmus test be applied to us all?

I remember the CEO of the above-mentioned company, at the annual meeting. I remember asking him what he meant by *integrity*, a word he bandied about—how he saw *integrity* operating in the company. "On a limbic level, Mr. President." He answered in bizspeak, which is like cheating in poker, if you want my opinion. So I feigned a cinematic episode of Tourette's Syndrome, *("Apres moi, Le deluge!"* I exclaimed) and then calmly asked him if he were aware crows could grasp the sophisticated concept of zero.

You don't have to be Zelig to be at the right place at the right time.

If each individual, at every junction, chose and chose well, there would have been no Rwanda. No orphans whispering, "We Live in a Country of Ghosts."

Bill Clinton had a choice that seminal April 7, 1994, when ten Belgian emissaries were killed trying to protect Prime Minister Agate Uwilingiyimana, who was dragged into the street and murdered. The ensuing violence spread like liquid.

I remember the news reports documenting the massive killings, but heard only spin from administration officials, determined to do nothing, fearing the sting of events in Somalia would loom in American minds.

From my window, the still streets of Cleveland Park appear almost sepulchral.

The sun is an auburn beauty, a Breck Girl.

We cannot revive the dead. I understand inside a glass case, somewhere, preserved, is a fax from Canadian General Romeo Dallaire, commander of a small U.N. peacekeeping force, pleading for U.S. help.

Received a telegram from Leon.
Maria is dead.

They wrapped her body in a clean muslin cloth.

They prayed for her under a sepia sky.

Leon is coming home with his daughter, Noel. I will meet them at Reagan National Airport at eleven o'clock.

The sun through my window is a blood-orange, dilating like a cervix.

Rwanda will make the history books, but the history of war is too important to be left to the historians.

Outside, wrens warble in the roof's carved eaves, and I imagine they weep.

Printed in the United States
75265LV00002B